Best of Wyldblood

Volume One

Edited by Mark Bilsborough

WYLDBLOOD

This edition published 2022 by Wyldblood Press, Thicket View, Maidenhead
SL6 6PX

© 2022 Wyldblood Press and contributors

All rights reserved. No part of this book may be reproduced, stored in a
retrieval system or transmitted by any means or in any form without the prior
written permission of the publisher.

ISBN: 978-1-914417-12-2

www.wyldblood.com

Contents

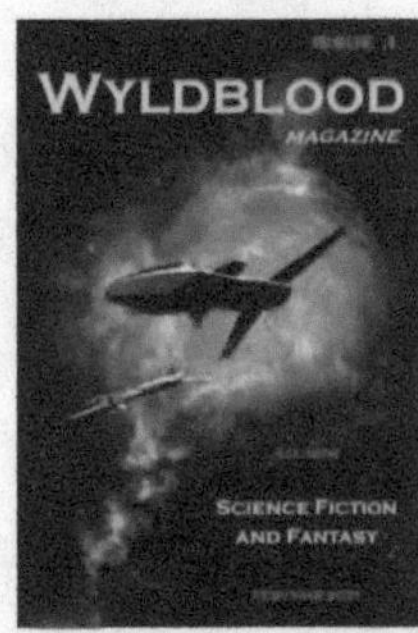

WYLDBLOOD
MAGAZINE
SCIENCE FICTION
AND FANTASY

WYLDBLOOD
MAGAZINE
FANTASY AND
SCIENCE FICTION

ISSUE 3
WYLDBLOOD
MAGAZINE
ALL NEW
SCIENCE FICTION
AND FANTASY

WYLDBLOOD
MAGAZINE
FANTASY AND
SCIENCE FICTION

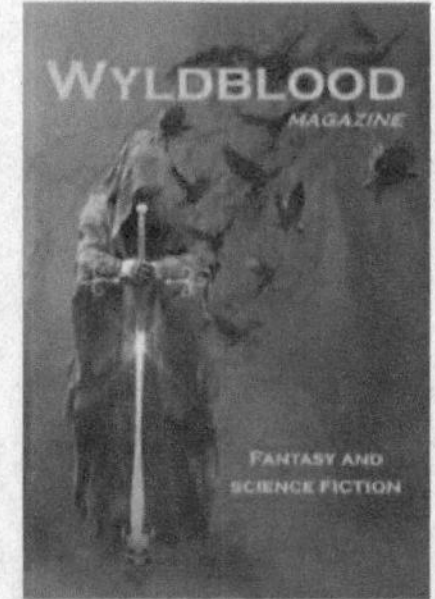

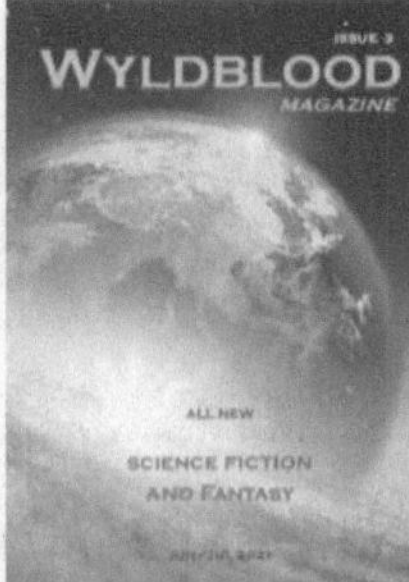

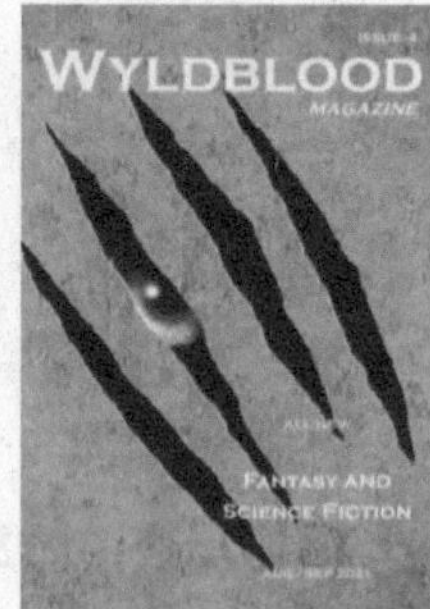

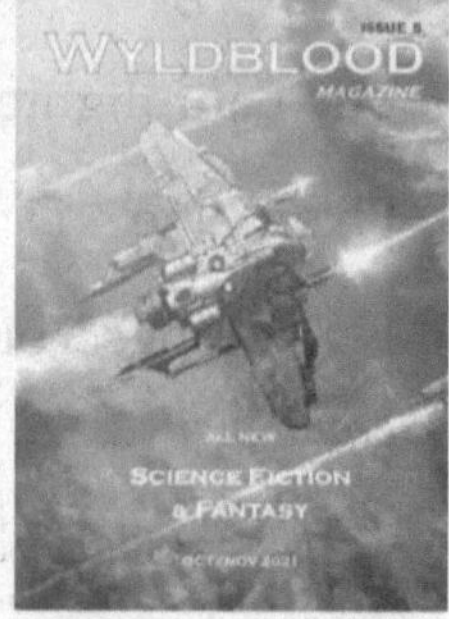

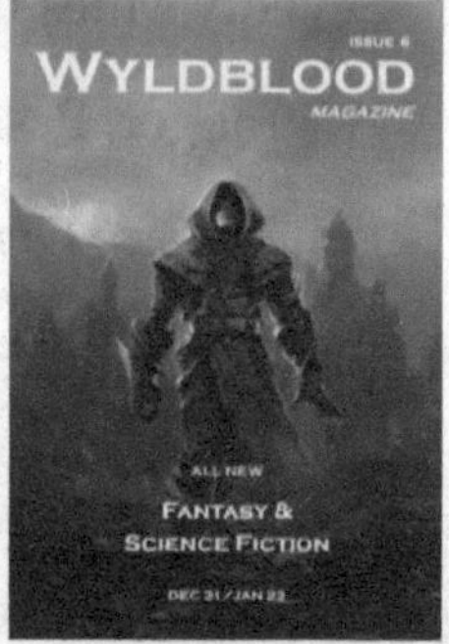

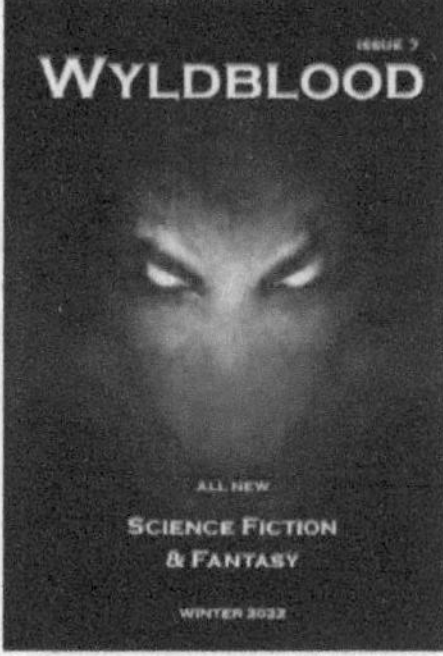

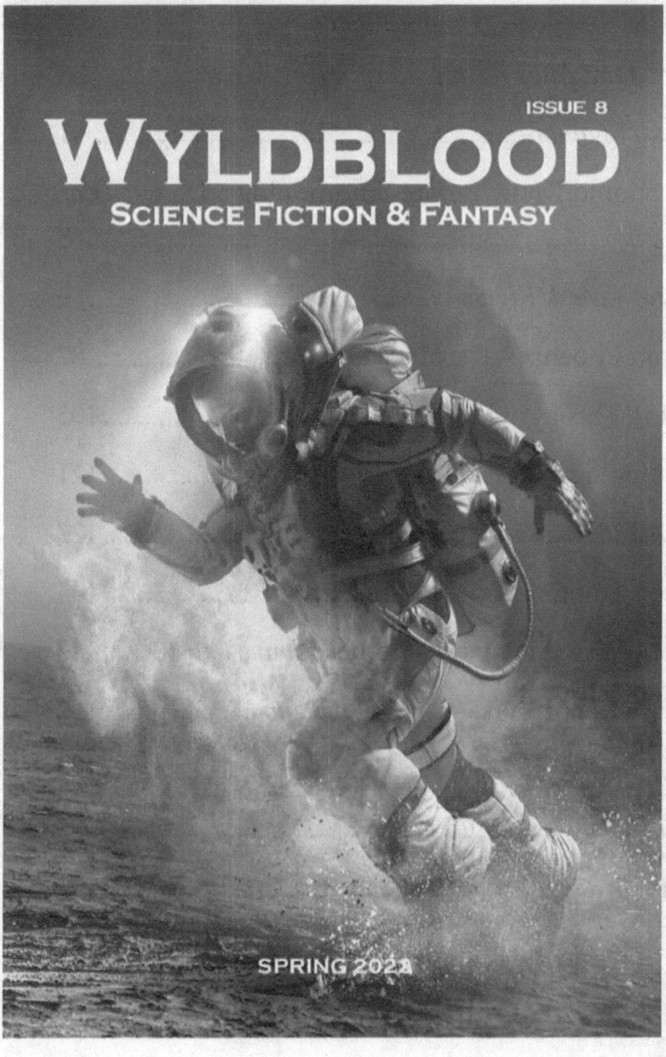
ISSUE 8
WYLDBLOOD
SCIENCE FICTION & FANTASY
SPRING 2022

ISSUE 5
WYLDBLOOD
MAGAZINE
ALL NEW
SCIENCE FICTION
& FANTASY
OCT/NOV 2021

ISSUE 6
WYLDBLOOD
MAGAZINE
ALL NEW
FANTASY &
SCIENCE FICTION
DEC 21 / JAN 22

ISSUE 7
WYLDBLOOD
ALL NEW
SCIENCE FICTION
& FANTASY
WINTER 2022

Introduction

When we started Wyldblood Press, in those dark and gloomy Lockdown days of 2020, we had no idea what would happen. Sure, we had a plan, involving books, magazines, free flash fiction and a growing community of dedicated writers. It was an ambitious plan, and relied on finding many fine stories from around the world.

I love it when a plan comes together.

As I write this, we've just published our tenth issue of Wyldblood, our anthology magazine which every three months showcases around ten new science fiction and fantasy stories. We've also put out a few themed anthologies: *Call of the Wyld,* where we got werewolves out of our system (until the full moon, of course) and *Runs Like Clockwork,* where we let ourselves go in the slightly unsettling world of steampunk. Sometime very soon we'll also have *From the Depths,* full of stories of the murky deep. And watch out for a series of novellas to be published in 2023, plus a couple of original novels to sit alongside the classic texts we've already published.

We've given you demons and dragons, astronauts and aliens and much more: one thing you can safely say about our writers is that they're imaginative. Talented, too. Most have been published in many places before, and will go on to be published in many more. But we're proud of our new writers too, and we know they'll go on to great things.

This collection is, we hope, the first of many and pulls together stories from our first eight issues plus a few Flash favourites. These are personal selections from the hundreds of stories we've published so far in our magazine and in our weekly *Wyld Flash* slot on our website. There are many more great stories we could have chosen, but they're all still available – our flash fiction is free to read online at www.wyldblood.com. And past issues of *Wyldblood* are also still available through the website, through Amazon or (by order) from bookstores.

We've got wide tastes, but we have got a house style – Wyldblood is the place for thoughtful, solidly written character-based stories, and we've got plenty in this collection, starting with Holley Cornetto's *Coal*

Dust and Shadows, the very first story from our very first issue, all about love, loss and ghosts. Further in, we've got an ice princess, a reluctant village guardian, a haunted mountain, demonology, killer robots, relentless trucks, ghosts old and new, alchemaic ink, time travel and magical tattoos.

In a changing, uncertain world, we need the foresight and vivid imagination of speculative fiction more than ever. There are stories of the apocalypse, of bad robots, dangerous aliens and climate disaster and we're proud to publish some, but just when we think there's no hope, that the planet-busting asteroid is about to hit us, maybe, just maybe, we can find a way.

Enjoy the stories,

Mark Bilsborough
Editor, Wyldblood Press

Coal Dust and Shadows
Holley Cornetto

Coal Dust and Shadows

A dense, uneasy fog had settled over the mountain the day they found the girl in the mine. It crept through hidden cracks and crevices of every home, bringing with it the unmistakable smell of earth and smoke.

Every miner who'd been there told the story differently. Some said she was behind a breakthrough, others that she'd been in an abandoned, half-caved section of the mine. Others still claimed she materialized out of thin air. The one thing they all agreed on is that she was lucky they found her when they did, because that entire section collapsed less than an hour after they extracted her.

My father said when they found her, she was just standing there, as if waiting for them. Her white cotton dress didn't have so much as a smudge on it, and she didn't speak a word.

When I saw her for the time in church on Sunday, I couldn't take my eyes off her. At seventeen years old, I'd never been in love before, but one look at her coal-black hair and pearly-white teeth was all it took. She looked like she'd stepped straight out of a fairy tale.

My little brother, Bobby, leaned close. "I heard she can't talk," he whispered, "and that she's retarded or something."

I punched his leg hard. "Shhh," I hissed. "Don't talk like that."

He wriggled back into the pew and sneered. Bobby didn't like being told what to do. He was two years younger, and we didn't get along well, but Momma always insisted I let him tag along with me.

When church dismissed, I begged Momma to introduce me to the girl from the mine. She gave me a look that was equal parts skeptical and amused. "Well, if she'll be staying in town, it might be nice for her to meet some other young people." She waved at Shane and Bobby. "Y'all come on, too."

Momma led us to the bench where the preacher's wife sat. Reverend Hancock and his wife didn't have children of their own, so they'd volunteered to take the girl in until other arrangements were made. As to what those arrangements might be, no one said.

"Shirley," Momma said, "I was wondering if you would introduce us to the young lady."

I looked down at my shoes, suddenly aware of my greasy hair and the dirt under my fingernails.

Mrs. Hancock smiled and placed a well-manicured hand on the girl's back. "This is Grace. Grace, this is Mrs. Hull, and her son Preston."

"Grace." I repeated, stepping forward.

Mrs. Hancock smiled. "Well, that's what we call her. A reminder to us all that she was saved from that mine by the grace of God."

Grace dipped her head politely in my direction.

I could see Bobby and Shane out of the corner of my eye. I tilted my head in their direction. "This is my brother, Bobby, and my best friend, Shane."

Before Bobby could cut in and embarrass me, Momma put a restraining hand on his shoulder. She shook her head at Mrs. Hancock. "It's a crying shame what happened. Has she said anything yet?"

"Naw, Grace here doesn't say anything at all."

Bobby poked me in the ribs, and turned his most earnest looking expression on Mrs. Hancock. "Can she understand what we say?"

I dug my heel into his foot. He grimaced, but didn't cry out.

Mrs. Hancock chuckled. "Yes, of course she can understand you. Ain't that right, Grace?"

Grace's eyes were as black as her hair. Eyes so deep I thought I might fall into them and keep falling forever. Words formed inside my mind: *I understand just fine.*

I searched her face for some evidence she'd spoken, but her mouth hadn't moved. I glanced over my shoulder at Bobby and Shane, but they looked bored. There was no indication she'd said anything at all, but her expression made clear she'd understood. I must've interpreted that look in my mind and imagined her speaking. My face burned hot.

Mrs. Hancock was still talking to Momma. "Doc Mason says it might be shock, and she may eventually speak again."

It's not shock.

The faint outline of a smile danced across her face as she looked in my direction. I didn't imagine the words. I might have been confused or afraid if I'd thought to question them, but all I could think was that she liked me, too. I cleared my throat and summoned courage I didn't know I had. "Would you mind if I come visit Grace after school tomorrow, Mrs. Hancock?"

"Well, I think that would be just fine, Preston. What do you think, Grace?"

Just fine. She nodded at Mrs. Hancock.

As we left church, Bobby danced in circles, taunting me. I hadn't expected any less from him. I thought Shane might understand, but he seemed preoccupied, muttering to himself with his head down. I caught the phrase "bad feeling" before the rest of his words were carried off by the wind.

I hesitated on the front porch of the Hancock's house, rehearsing what I would say. Before I could knock, the door swung open and Grace emerged in her white cotton dress. I got the feeling she'd been waiting for me. I inhaled sharply, forgetting how to use words.

She smiled and walked down the steps, and I stumbled after her. "I don't know how to ask, but..." I rubbed the back of my neck. "Yesterday, at church... I thought you were talking to me. Like I could hear you in my head or something." I cringed. That didn't come out the way I'd intended.

She answered with a smile.

"Can you read my mind?"

Of course not.

"There! That! Did you do that? You answered me, didn't you?"

She dipped her head in a nod.

"Do you do that with other people? Can you?"

Just you.

I knew I looked like an idiot, but I couldn't stop the ear-to-ear grin from spreading across my face. "I can show you around town. If you want to, I mean."

She smiled again, and my heart sped up in my chest.

Every day after school, I found her sitting on the porch waiting for me. Some days we walked together in silence; on others I asked her questions. Sometimes, she even answered.

By the following week, we'd fallen into a routine. When I arrived, she stood and looked at me with those coal black eyes. My hands trembled. That much hadn't changed.

Show me the mines.

"Are you sure?" I'd been avoiding taking her there. Baylor had been a mining town for as long as anyone could remember, but I preferred fresh air and sunshine. The thought of being underground nauseated me. It was too confining. When I turned eighteen, everyone expected me to get a job in the mines as my father had done, and his father before him. But I didn't care that mining was the family trade. I wanted no part of it.

She placed her hands on her hips and tilted her head.

"All right, all right." I lifted my hands in surrender and took a step back. "I know a place with a view of the whole mountain. It's a bit of a hike, though, so let me grab some supplies before we go."

We arrived at Hawk's Nest about an hour and a half later. When we reached the clearing, I removed the faded quilt I'd taken from my bedroom, spreading it on the ground for her to sit.

"What do you think? You can see pretty much everything from here."

She was looking toward the mine's entrance in the distance, her brow furrowed.

"Grace?"

They are going to expand it. Drill deeper.

"Yeah." I settled in beside her on the blanket. "That's what I heard, too."

Her jaw was clenched, and I couldn't tell if the shine in her eyes was anger or sadness.

They shouldn't be digging so deep. They're disturbing things they don't understand.

Her words caught me off guard. "Do you mean there's something down there? Did you see something when you were inside?" I thought about taking her hand, about how it would feel in mine.

The mountain was here long before this town, or the people in it. Just because it can't walk or talk doesn't mean it has no spirit, or that it can't feel.

Despite the heat of the West Virginia sun, her words made my blood run cold. "I feel that way too, when I'm out in the forest and there's a stand of old trees. I think sometimes about how long those trees have been there. Longer than I've been alive, or my parents. Longer than my grandparents, even."

She shook her head, but didn't say more.

I put my hand down on the blanket beside hers, just close enough that our fingertips brushed together. "Can I tell you a secret?"

She tilted her head toward me.

"I hate those damned mines. I'd do anything to not have to work in them when I'm older."

Do you have to?

"It's tradition. All the boys in Baylor work the mines when they turn eighteen." I inched my fingers toward her. She didn't move hers away.

You don't want to, though.

I shook my head, and slid my hand over hers. "I'd rather be a farmer. I want to work out in the open air and sunshine."

Her arm jerked, and I cursed myself for a fool. I started to apologize, but stopped when I saw her body convulsing.

I caught her before she collapsed onto the ground. Her eyes rolled back and her body tremored, as if she were having a seizure. I turned her head sideways, and cursed myself for bringing her out here. The climb was probably too much for her.

A loud boom like the crack of thunder sounded below, cascading over the hills and up the mountain. I saw men spill from mine like ants from a hill, shouting and running, chased by pillars of smoke. There was another boom, and a black cloud of dust obscured my view.

By the time the smoke and dust cleared, Grace lay still in my lap.

I worried that I wouldn't be able to carry her back down the path, but when I lifted her, she was as light as a shadow.

It was full dark by the time I carried Grace up the stairs to the Hancocks' house. Mrs. Hancock pulled Grace out of my arms and yelled for her husband. They brought her inside, leaving me on the front porch. I sat on the old wooden steps and settled in to wait.

I don't know how long I'd been sitting when the door swung open and Reverend Hancock emerged. He startled when he saw me. "Preston?"

I stood and dusted off my pants leg. "Yes, sir?"

"What are you doing out here? I thought you'd gone home."

I looked past him into the open doorway, but there was no sign of her. "I wanted to make sure Grace was alright."

"There's nothing you can do for her right now. Why don't you go on home, and come back in a day or two, after she's had time to rest?"

I nodded reluctantly and started down the path toward home.

Shane and Bobby caught up with me after school the next day.

"You going to visit your girlfriend again?" Shane asked. "I ain't seen you all week."

Bobby slapped at my books, trying to knock them from my hands. I lifted them overhead where he couldn't reach them. "Naw, she's sick."

"Sick of you, maybe!" Bobby said, jumping to try and tip the books from my hand.

"What's wrong with her?" Shane frowned at Bobby, then stepped forward and shoved him lightly. "Knock it off, twerp."

"Jerk."

"Butt-face."

"She wanted to see the mines," I interrupted, "so I took her up to Hawk's Nest. While we were there, she had a seizure or something."

Bobby thrust his hips. "Was it like this? 'Cause that's an orgasm, dipshit!"

Shane smirked and slapped Bobby on the back of the head. "I don't know why we put up with you." He turned back to me. "Did you hear about the explosion?"

I nodded. "I saw it, actually. I didn't know what it was, though. It happened at the same time Grace started freaking out, so I didn't get a good look. I just heard the boom and saw clouds of smoke and ash."

Shane lifted a brow. "Well, if you ain't gonna see her today, you and me and Bobby ought to go to Clear Creek."

"I'll meet you there." I said, and turned onto the dirt road that led home.

We met at our usual spot, where large, weathered stones lay scattered in the creek bed. We'd spent many hot summer days here swimming and daring each other to jump across the rocks.

Shane lifted a small round stone, bouncing it to test its weight in his palm. "We thought you'd got sick of us." For Shane, conversation was like haggling. He started with an unlikely proposition, then worked his way toward the heart of the matter.

Bobby jumped in and sent a spray of water in my direction. "Your girlfriend's a freak! She only likes you because she's soft in the head."

I clenched my fists and started after him, but Shane grabbed my shoulder. "Let it go. You know how he is, he's just talking shit."

Shane offered me the stone in his hand. I took it and flipped my wrist in one fluid motion, sending it skimming across the water's surface.

"So, you really like her, huh?" He tossed another stone in after mine. He looked out across the water, counting the times it bounced off the surface.

It was an unspoken rule not to look each other in the eyes when we talked about something serious or embarrassing. Given the heat on my cheeks, I was grateful for the rule. "I do."

"How d'you know you like her if she never says anything? I mean, she's pretty and all, but don't you get bored with all the silence?"

I glanced across the water and spotted Bobby upstream, using my shoe to catch minnows. I pretended not to notice. The last thing I needed was for him to overhear. "There's something I wanna tell you, and I don't know if you're going to believe me. It sounds crazy."

Shane sent another stone skipping across the surface. "You know I'll believe you. You don't lie. Hell, you don't even exaggerate."

"She *does* talk to me."

Despite our rule, Shane turned to me in surprise. "You mean she's been able to talk all this time and--"

"No. Not like that. I mean, she says things *in my head*." Unable to meet his eyes, I studied the stone in my hand.

"Preston…" From the corner of my eye, I could see him glance upstream. Satisfied that Bobby was out of listening range, he continued, "What does 'in my head' mean exactly?"

I ran my thumb along the rock's smooth surface. "I can hear her… in my head. But her lips don't move, and no one else can hear it."

Shane ran a hand through his hair. "Are you trying to tell me she's telepathic?"

"I… I don't know." I sat down on the boulder, dangling my feet in the water. "I asked her, and she said she can't read my mind, or anything weird like that."

Shane chuckled. "Right, because *that* would be weird."

I suddenly realized how ridiculous it sounded, and I laughed with him. "You aren't going to call me insane?"

He rubbed his chin. "I told you I'd believe you, and I do. But I don't know what, exactly, I'm believing here. There's definitely something strange about her. You remember the seizure you told me about?"

"Yeah."

"Well, that ain't the first one she's had. My daddy said she had some kinda fit after they pulled her out of the mine. Shaking and foaming at the mouth. Right around the time the shaft they found her in collapsed."

I dropped a stone into the water. What he was implying didn't make sense. "What are you trying to say?"

"I don't know. Just… something is weird about all this. Before she showed up, do you know how long it had been since there were any big accidents at the mine? Twenty years. Twenty! But after she shows up, suddenly there are two major accidents in a week. It ain't normal, Preston."

Shane prided himself on knowing everything there was to know about the town's history. He couldn't wait for the day he was old enough to plunge into the depths of the mountain and baptize himself in its darkness. If he said twenty years, I believed him.

"Hey!" Bobby yelled. "Are y'all gonna come swimming or not?"

I shook my head. "I think I should head home. Give me back my shoe, asshole."

He waded further into the creek, holding my shoe over his head.

I grumbled under my breath and headed in after him.

I couldn't concentrate the next day at school. I kept one eye on the clock, and tried to calm the butterflies in my stomach. Around one thirty, Vice Principal Childers came in and called several students out of class. Usually stern from breaking up too many fights over the years, Childers showed no trace of anger, only concern. The entire class seemed to hold their breath as he listed off the names. Shane was called second to last.

I knew only one thing could have affected that many students. When the bell rang for dismissal, I jumped from my desk and ran straight to Shane's house.

His little sister was on the front porch when I arrived. I doubled over, trying to catch my breath.

"Are you looking for Shane?"

"Yeah, he got called out of school. Is everything okay? Is he here?" My t-shirt clung to pools of sweat on my back. I used the collar to dry my forehead.

"He's inside. I'll get him. You don't want to go in there." She vanished behind the screen door.

Her words sent a shiver down my spine. A thousand scenarios ran through my mind. Maybe I was wrong and there wasn't another accident. Maybe someone was sick. Contagious.

The door creaked, interrupting my speculation. Shane stepped onto the porch. He looked tired, drained. "Preston." Something in his tone made me feel like an intruder.

"You left school today. I was worried."

"There was another accident at the mine." His eyes flickered upward. "Daddy and some of his crew got trapped inside."

It felt like the wind had been knocked out of me. "Are they... alive?"

"They don't know yet. They're drilling, trying to break through and make contact." Unshed tears glinted from the corners of his eyes.

"Shit, Shane, I'm so sorry."

"Have you seen Grace today?" The muscles of his jaw tightened when he said her name.

"No, I came straight here. Why?"

"Because, I want to know if she had another one of her damned fits! I want to know if she did this!"

"Shane, that's…"

"Impossible? You're the one that told me she spoke to you in your head." He jabbed his finger into my collarbone. "She's some kind of witch, or demon, or God-knows-what, and I want to know if she made this happen."

"How could she? She's just a girl, Shane. And a sick one, at that." He wasn't thinking clearly. He was upset about the accident. He needed someone to blame, and he'd picked Grace.

"You go see her, Preston. See if she's still sick. Then come back here and tell me she didn't do this."

If I couldn't reason with him, I could at least see Grace to prove his theory wrong. "Okay, I'll go."

For a moment, I thought I'd only imagined her sitting on the steps. The angle of the sun blanketed her in shadow, leaving her little more than a silhouette. "Grace?"

When I spoke her name, it was as if those shadows took tangible form, and she was again herself. But that was silly, just my imagination playing tricks. A large basket sat beside her, and as I glanced at it, she pushed it aside.

Not yet. It's a surprise.

For a moment, she almost made me forget my promise to Shane. "So, then… you're well today? You didn't have another seizure or anything?"

My fever broke this afternoon. I woke up and felt fine.

"What time did you wake up?"

She looked up at me, and I saw myself reflected in her eyes. She scooted away just slightly, and crossed her arms over her chest.

"I'm sorry. I should've said I'm glad you're okay." I offered her my hand.

She lifted the basket and took my hand. This time she led me, taking me down to the path toward the creek. She took the long way; one I didn't often travel. I noticed the soles of her feet flashed black when she walked, as if covered in coal dust.

We stopped at a thicket of mountain laurels, where she spread a blanket and unpacked the picnic she'd prepared. I watched her unpack fried chicken, coleslaw, and lemonade. All my favorite things, though I'd never told her. I wondered for a moment if she'd lied about reading my mind.

"Grace, there's something I need to ask you."

She nodded and took my hands in hers, pulling me down to join her on the blanket. The sunlight glimmered off the white dress she always wore.

I settled in beside her and shook away my distraction. I had to make good on my promise to Shane. "Do you know anything about the accidents at the mine?"

Her lip quivered. *I thought you hated the mines.*

It was neither confirmation nor denial. I'd have to approach the subject another way. I took a bite of the chicken. "Thanks for this," I said after swallowing. "You got all my favorites."

By the time we finished our picnic, the sky was growing dark. She scooted closer and took my hand.

There were so many things I needed to ask her - about the mountain and the mines, about her seizures and her fever, about how she knew my favorite things to eat. But before I could organize my thoughts into words, she took my cheek in her hand and leaned forward.

As we kissed, my questions dissolved. All words were lost to me, useless to express the things I felt. A thick fog seeped from the earth to shroud us in its curtain, shutting out the world.

Some might've called what we did a sin, and if it was a sin, it was one born of love. Afterward, I lay on the blanket beside her, my nose pressed against her hair, breathing in her scent of earth and smoke. My heart felt as though it would burst. I couldn't remember a time when I'd ever been so happy.

I wrapped my arms around her as if she were some phantom girl who might, at any moment, become a part of the fog that surrounded us. In that moment, I knew I had lied to Shane. She wasn't *just* a girl.

She was something else entirely. "Grace," I whispered, "tell me about the mines."

They come with their drills and bring destruction.

"I know, but those men are innocent."

I thought you hated the mine too, I thought you'd understand.

There was a bitterness in her tone that caught me off guard. It was cold and hard, like the mountain.

"They do what they must to provide for their families." There was more I wanted to say, but the heavy fog surrounding us made my head feel light.

She settled in against me, and we lay together in quiet stillness until I fell into the blackest depths of a dreamless sleep.

I couldn't tell how long I slept, but when I woke, the blanket beside me was empty. I sat bolt upright and looked around the laurel thicket, but saw no sign of Grace. I grabbed my clothes and pulled them on with shaking hands. I trembled not with cold, I realized, but with fear.

"Grace?" I took a few steps toward the edge of the laurels.

Silence.

Maybe she was afraid of being caught out late and snuck home. The more I thought about it, the more it made sense to me. She'd tried to wake me but couldn't. Or, maybe she wanted me to rest.

When I got back to our picnic site, I noticed that her side of the blanket was covered with a fine layer of black dust.

I woke the next morning in my own bed, my head pounding out the rhythm of my heartbeat. My sheets were caked with grime and dried blood. Cuts covered my legs from groping my way home in the darkness. I didn't remember walking home. I must have, but I couldn't remember.

The telephone's high-pitched ring made my head feel as if it were splitting. I stumbled into the kitchen and lifted the receiver. It was Shane.

"They got them out, Preston. They're all going to be okay."

The miners. Memories of yesterday's events flooded back. "I talked to Grace about the accidents. I don't think you need to worry anymore."

"Grace?" He asked.

He must've forgotten in all the excitement. "Yeah. Remember yesterday? You said you thought that she… might have something to do with the accident."

"Who's Grace?"

My heart sank. It wasn't like him to play pranks, especially considering what he'd been through these past few days.

"Look Preston, I'm sorry, but I need to go. I have more calls to make. Talk to you, later."

"Yeah, later," I tried to answer, but he'd already hung up. I stared at the phone in my hand as if it could give me answers.

"Who was that on the phone?"

I jumped at the sound of my mother's voice. "Shane. He said they rescued the men who were trapped."

She filled a mug with coffee and sat down at the table, patting the place beside her. "I heard. Your father went to visit the hospital this morning. But that's where the good news ends, I'm afraid."

"What do you mean?"

"An inspector came in to investigate the recent accidents. They've decided the best course of action is to close the mines."

My head pounded with the echo of Grace's words, but in a voice I did not recall. It was an ancient sound, a deep rumble like shifting gravel. *I thought you'd understand.*

"Grace."

Momma tilted her head. "What, honey?"

"Grace. She hated those mines."

She shook her head. "Who is Grace?"

"The girl they pulled out of the mine. The girl staying with the Hancocks. We met her at church, remember?"

"They didn't pull any girl out of the mine. Not that I know of, anyway. When did you say this happened?"

"Just last week, Mom."

She pressed the back of her hand against my forehead. "Do you feel alright?"

"I'm fine."

"You're burning up. I think you must've had a fever dream." She led me back to my bedroom and tsked when she saw the dirty sheets. "I'll never understand how you boys are always so filthy!" I sat on the trunk at the foot of my bed while she grabbed fresh linens.

Why would Mom and Shane act like they didn't know Grace? Why pretend she never existed?

Mom turned down the bed and held up the blanket. "Get settled in. I'll bring you something to bring the fever down."

I nodded. I hoped I was dreaming, that I'd wake up and find myself still in the laurel thicket with Grace. I closed my eyes, and fell into a fitful sleep.

Each time I woke, someone different stood over me: Doc Mason, my parents, Shane, Bobby. I tried to ask about Grace, but no one answered. No one remembered.

The doctor was sitting at the edge of the bed when I came around. "You had us all worried for a while there, young man." His tone was matter-of-fact. "You've had a severe fever, and hallucinations."

"Hallucinations?" I asked.

"You kept asking for someone named Grace."

I swallowed. The inside of my mouth was like a desert.

"You may be weak for a day or two longer, so take it easy until you feel like yourself again." He patted my knee, and left me to my thoughts.

Eventually, I recovered. No one spoke of the hallucinations again. When I tried to bring it up with my mom, she simply said I was sick, and it couldn't be helped.

No one remembered Grace. After a while, I began to wonder whether or not she had been real. Even now, when I try to conjure her image in my mind's eye, her form darkens and shifts as if she weren't of flesh and bone. As if she were made of coal dust and shadows

Holley Cornetto has stories in or forthcoming in over a dozen magazines and anthologies, including: Daily Science Fiction (2020), It Calls From the Forest (2020),

Holley Cornetto

Scare Me (2020), and *The Half That You See: Nightmares, Deliriums, and Illusions* .(2021), among others.

Thawing
JL George

Thawing

The ice princess watched over us from her plinth in the city square, crystalline, inviolate, and perfect.

The first time I saw her, I was a child, tugging restlessly at my father's hand as we waited for Mother to finish up her business in the city. The day had dragged on longer than expected, forcing him to spend money on hot tea and handcakes from the vendors who lined the square. My ears were cold and I was tired of walking, grizzling and complaining endlessly—until the clouds parted and allowed through a pale beam of winter sun that glittered on her face.

I stopped, transfixed, and Father hoisted me into his arms, glad of the distraction. "Did I tell you the story of Princess Eira?" he said. "No? Well, it's about time I did."

A long time ago, the tale began, the city of Dinas Uchaf and the lands around it had been ruled by kings and queens. Over time, their power diminished, and the elders of the city made most of the decisions, but their descendants continued to live in the palace. They gave the inhabitants something to be proud of, Father explained. They were a living reminder of our heritage, our traditions.

Princess Eira had been wise, and kind, and discontented with sitting in the palace wearing fine silk dresses and putting in appearances at state events and galas. She took to walking among the people in ordinary clothes, talking with them in the streets, and they, all unknowing who she was, spilled their troubles to her as they did to their neighbours. And then she took to petitioning the Council of Elders, begging for help for the poor and the hungry, giving her own wealth to feed and clothe them and send their children to school. The people adored her.

But there was another problem. The ice dragons of the north moved ever closer to the city, encroaching on the outlying villages with their frozen breath that killed the crops, decimating the farmers' herds with their talons like knives of ice. Dinas Uchaf had always been cold, with snow on the ground even in summer, but the dragons threatened to make it an uninhabitable wasteland. All the fighting men and women of Dinas Uchaf couldn't hold them back. They would retreat only if offered a sacrifice.

Eira knew what she had to do. She rode forth beyond the city walls—for in those days it had been a fortress, much smaller than today's sprawl and bounded in on all sides—into what was now the square. There she came face to face with the greatest and fiercest of the dragons. The ground froze where his feet touched it and his breath, glittering with ice crystals, deadened the trees. Eira lowered her eyes, accepting her fate, and with a single exhalation he froze her solid where she stood.

She has stood here ever since, watching over Dinas Uchaf and its people. They say that should the ice ever melt, the city will fall and the ice dragons come howling back to claim it.

Father winked at me, then. "That's what they say, anyway. It's only a statue. Still, better not touch it, hm? The custodian'll tell us off."

I nodded, but my eyes lingered on the ice princess's face, its expression of stoic acceptance, the unseeing crystals of her eyes. To have stood there untouched, for so many years. She must have been so terribly lonely.

Each time my parents took me to the city, after that, I begged to be allowed to see the ice princess. And each time, they smiled and let me stand at the foot of the statue, my hands hot inside my gloves, knowing the statue would melt were I to touch it, and itching to do so anyway.

They assumed the fascination would fade as I grew older, but it never did. I wore out my friends with staring at her when they were more interested in visiting the stalls around the square or flirting with the sons and daughters of the market traders. My ambition was one thing only: to become custodian of the square, so that one day I should be the one to take care of her, to sweep the snow from the steps around her statue and tell her story to staring children.

Mother and Father thought it a child's fancy, at first, but it did not pass, and when I reached an age to leave home, they sent me to the city to be apprenticed.

Old Anna, the custodian, was brisk at first, barking at me for daydreaming when I paused too long to gaze upon the ice princess.

But as the months wore on her demeanour softened. "You're a hardworking lass, I'll give you that," she allowed, at first. And a few months later: "You care for her, don't you? The princess?"

I held myself still, fearing she'd seen something unseemly in my attachment to the statue. It was a thing I held close to my chest, fearing that the light of scrutiny might melt it like a snowflake on the tongue. "That's our job," I said.

Anna lifted an eyebrow. The effect, on her weather-beaten face, was that of someone having drawn a sceptical expression on a brown paper bag. "Don't come that with me," she said. "And don't talk like it's something to be ashamed of. Princess needs her guardian, and that can't be me much longer. My bones ache in the cold." She flexed an arthritic hand for emphasis, knuckles cracking.

My heart leapt. That night I sat up late in the square, the snow settling on my hair and my shoulders, and talked to the ice princess. "I think old Anna means to retire soon," I told her. "Will you miss her, I wonder?" I frowned and tipped my head back. The clouds had parted to reveal the Pole Star, bright and lonely and terribly far away. "She'll miss you. I know that."

The ice princess stayed where she was, that same immovable expression on her face. The longer I spent around her, the harder I found it to read. When I was young, listening to Father's stories, I'd thought it the quiet acceptance of somebody resigned to her fate. Now I imagined the hint of a smile in it sometimes; other days, an incipient frown.

I imagined her eyes followed me across the square as I returned to the custodian's hut, tracing the trail of my footprints in the snow; but when I turned back, at the last, her gaze was fixed blankly upon her folded hands.

Old Anna retired at the midwinter solstice, saying it was a new year, and time for a new custodian. My parents came to the city to celebrate my promotion. We ate lunch in a real restaurant, and I drank a cup of wine that stained my lips and made my head feel light and expansive.

As I returned to my bed, I saw a figure in the square, near the ice princess. I opened my mouth to shout, but then I recognized the stooped form: Anna, taking her leave.

I stepped back into the shadows of the square, aware I was intruding on something private. Anna lingered by the statue—talking to her, perhaps, though too quietly for me to hear. She reached up, then, and placed her hand lightly on the clasped ones of the princess.

My breath caught in my throat. Never touch her with bare hands. Your warm skin will melt the ice. I'd known that since I was small. It had been the first lesson Anna had drilled into me, too, and I'd been scrupulous in observing it. Yet here she was, her ungloved hand curling around the statue's as though she was taking her leave of an old friend.

I waited, holding my breath, for Anna to leave. She would stay with her nephew and his wife tonight, now the custodian's hut was no longer hers. It might take her a while to find a place in the city that her pension would cover. She'd talked about going south, back to the farming village where she and her sisters had been born, where the air was clean and the streets quiet. I hoped she would be happy, wherever she went.

Back in the custodian's hut—my hut, now—I curled up beneath my blankets and slept fitfully. Perhaps it was the wine, or perhaps the hut was too quiet for comfort without Anna's stertorous breathing. My dreams were sharp and strange.

The ice princess at night, but this time it was I and not Anna who reached out to take her hand. The ice princess toppling from her pedestal and smashing to smithereens on the flagstones. The ice princess, but not made of ice at all. She was a living woman with pink cheeks and yellow hair, and she reached for my hand and murmured, "Call me Eira."

I leaned in toward her, but before our lips touched, the dream broke and I woke shivering. I had forgotten to close the window last night, and there were snowflakes clinging to my eyelashes.

Late the next day, the last few stallholders closing up shop in the square, I brushed the snowflakes from the ice princess's shoulders. I'd never thought of it before, but using the brush felt impersonal, distant. Before last night, how long had it been since somebody had touched her?

I chided myself for the thought. She was only a statue, after all. The real Eira had given her life for the city many years ago.

But before I left to secure the barriers that would protect her for the night, I laid my gloved hand softly on her shoulder.

She did not turn to water on the spot, as some irrational part of me had feared. She stayed as she had always been: cold, unmoving, lonely.

I dreamed of her again that night. In the dream, she stood in sunshine, wearing a dress that bared her freckled shoulders, and her skin was warm beneath my hand. At my touch, she turned to face me, her eyes full of sorrow.

"I've been trapped here so long," she said. "It's so cold."

"What can I do?" I heard myself say.

She placed her palm against mine, interlacing our fingers. "You know what to do," she told me.

"I can't," I said. "You'll melt, you'll vanish."

Eira put her head on one side. "Who told you that?"

It took me a while to pluck up the courage. Weeks of brief, hesitant touches with gloved hands after dark; weeks of the same dream, where Eira urged me to set her free and I protested.

I told myself it was my imagination. Without old Anna around to ground me, my mind was playing tricks on itself. The ice princess in the square was only a memorial. Perhaps if I visited the real Eira's grave, it would set my mind to rest.

The next time my father came to the city, we sat at the foot of the statue drinking hot tea, and I broached the subject with him. "You remember when I was small? And we were right here, and you told me the story of Princess Eira?"

Father smiled, the wrinkles at the corners of his eyes creasing up. "Of course. I could never get you to concentrate for two minutes at a time, but that story? You listened to the whole thing without so much as looking away."

"But you didn't tell me everything."

He frowned. "What do you mean?"

"The ice princess—the real princess, I mean. Princess Eira. What happened to her? I mean, where did they bury her?"

"You know, I don't think I know. One of the old crypts under the city, I suppose."

Mother didn't know, either. Neither did old Anna, when she next came into the city to visit her nephew. Neither had the elders of the city council who paid my wages, or any of the visitors who stopped before the statue to tell their own children Eira's story.

The next time I had the dream, I took a deep breath and asked her, "What did you mean? When you asked who told me about the statue?"

She took both my hands in hers. "I meant what I said. Where did it come from, that story? Who does it serve?"

"It came from my father. And he heard it from his parents, and I suppose they heard it from theirs." I shrugged. "It's an old tale. Everybody knows it."

"Everybody knows," she echoed, "yet none of them were there." She looked into my eyes. "And my other question? Who does it serve?"

I shook my head. "I don't understand. It's just a story about how the city came to be."

"Every origin story serves somebody," Eira said. "Think about who's telling it. Who isn't here to speak."

"You."

"Me. I'm frozen in time. Voiceless. And the story ensures I stay that way. The ice melts, the dragons return. And we wouldn't want that, would we?" Her voice hardened, an unfamiliar, sardonic twist to her mouth.

"But nobody really believes that," I pointed out. "It's a statue, in the square. Even children know. Father told me so when I was little."

"And yet the city pays you to ensure that the ice never melts. That the dragons never return."

"They're not real," I said. "It's just a story."

"It's just *half* a story."

The humans had won; the ice dragons had left. The story said that it was peaceful, and right. Of course, nobody had seen a dragon near human habitation in a hundred years. We couldn't have asked them if we'd wanted to.

I almost didn't dare ask; but I had to. "What really happened?"

"Walk with me."

Eira took my hand, and in the dream, we wound our way between young trees with lemons ripening on their branches, the lush grass soft beneath our feet. I'd never seen such things in the waking world. This had to be somewhere down south, nowhere near Dinas Uchaf.

"The dragons were here before us," Eira said, at length. "Their migrations last for years, and in their absence, humans found this place and built a city on it. But it had been their home for thousands of years. Hundreds of thousands."

I blinked. "I didn't know that."

"Nor did I, until I was old enough that Father gave me free rein in his library. I went straight for the histories that were censored elsewhere, of course." She gave a short, bitter laugh. "The dragons had begun to be an issue—that was how they put it—when I was very small. I'd grown up hearing adults bicker over how we should deal with the problem. Imagine my surprise when I learned that *we* were the problem, not them!"

I didn't need to imagine it. I supposed my expression gave that away. Eira went on, her eyes distant. "Imagine my even greater surprise when my father—my kind, gentle father—advised me to tell no-one of what I'd learned. It didn't matter, he said. This was our home now. The dragons had chosen to leave it behind; they could hardly return and claim it again."

"But they tried."

"They did. And I couldn't keep silent forever. After Father died, I begged the Council of Elders to talk to them. To bargain. Even to abandon the city and rebuild anew in the south! They refused, and so I took my concerns before the people."

"The people loved you," I said, recalling what Father had told me. "That part was true, at least?"

"Many of them did. Some disagreed. There was great division in the city, and the dragons were upon us, and I did not know what to do. But the council of elders had an idea."

Her expression darkened and she fell silent. I squeezed her hand in encouragement.

"They managed to capture a small dragon. A juvenile; the offspring of the leader. They threatened to kill her if the dragons did not leave the city to stand. And, to ensure they stayed away, they demanded their participation in a binding magic. A spell that would keep them from the city as long as it lasted." Her voice trembled, just briefly. "It did, I'm afraid, require a sacrifice. And there was somebody they very much desired to get out of the way."

Her eyes brimmed with tears, and mine did, too. The city I'd longed to live in, the statue I'd longed to protect—it had been a lie. All of it, a lie.

Eira took my face in her hands. "Your parents don't live in the city."

I shook my head. "They fish. They live on the coast, to the southeast."

"Good. Then you have a place to run to."

"Run…?"

"You know what to do," she said, and pressed her lips to mine; and this time it was true.

This time, I was running across the square before I was even fully conscious I was awake.

The early-morning walkers looked at me strangely, but I spared them not a moment's thought. I made for the statue.

No: for the ice princess.

I wrapped my arms around her and pressed kisses to her lips, and felt the ice begin to melt at my touch.

Above the city, a cold crack of lightning. Fear coiled in my chest as I raised my eyes and saw the blizzard that was coming, the great shapes, diamond-white, that roiled within it.

Somebody took my hand.

I whirled, and there she was, standing beside me. A princess of flesh and blood and warmth and rage, free at last from her cold prison. She surveyed the city around her.

"Eira?" My voice wavered.

"Let it freeze," she said, at last.

The storm was upon us now, and hand in hand, we ran.

JL George

JL George *is based in Cardiff and has work featured or forthcoming in Fireside, Writers of the Future, Constellary Tales, and various other magazines and anthologies.*

The Lamplighter's Daughter
Anne Karppinen

Anne Karppinen

The Lamplighter's Daughter

The day is getting darker. The sun has set, and the deep, velvety sky is illuminated only by the smallest sliver of a moon. Shadows stretch out from behind the stones, turning the snow into deeper shades of blue. Trees rattle their branches. There's ice in the air – death, too, for those too slow to find shelter. There's a merciless beauty to this weather, something very few people ever get to see, or even know how to look for.

I raise the lantern, trying to cast its glow as far ahead of me as possible. But it's useless: there's nothing to see here, nothing to show. I'd know my way back by the feel of the path beneath my feet and by the smell of smoke from the village. I could make this journey with my eyes closed. There are days when I've done so. The lantern isn't here to guide me or to keep me safe: it serves quite another purpose.

I follow the path down to the village. Houses, their walls prickled with ice, hunch against the darkness, spouting smoke from their chimneys in unison. I can hear pans clanging in the kitchens, plates being scraped, somebody singing a baby to sleep. Water dripping from wet socks over fireplaces. Life going on as life should: mundanely, repetitively, unfurling in slow circles.

Now and then there's a silence: people stop and hear my footsteps. I walk louder than necessary, just to jolt them out of their routines – just to give them a small taste of uncertainty after dinner. Behind a bolted gate, a guard dog bursts into loud barking. I greet it by name, and the dog purses its mouth, confused. It pads over to the doorstep and lies down, a coil of soft fur and pointed ears. Behind the door, people let out a sigh and resume their meal. Now, the dog has a good reason to be on its guard, locked as it is in the dark yard by itself. But the people indoors, with their firelight and bright lamps – why are they so easily startled? Surely they recognise my footfall by now: I walk the same route every day, checking all the lanterns on the way and topping up their oil. I'm beginning to agree with my father: fear can be a delicious thing, if sampled in small quantities and tempered with the feeling of immediate safety.

I make sure to extinguish the lamp before I reach our gate; such brightness feels excessive in our small home. For us, darkness is a relief after a day's toil: it requires nothing of us but silence and rest. In his forgetfulness, father has latched the front door from the inside. I bang on the kitchen shutter, not caring if anyone hears.

'No need to make such a racket.' I hear my father's voice through the double doors. As he pushes open the outer one, he adds, 'Sometimes I think the gods gave me a son in the shape of a daughter, I really do.' He crinkles his hairy face and shuts the door swiftly behind me. 'Any luck?'

'No,' I reply, stomping snow off my boots.

'But it's not luck, really, is it? The fish, like the signs, arrive just when we need them most.' He rests his hand briefly on my shoulder as he squeezes past me in the dim corridor. 'You must be hungry.'

Father watches me eat. He says he's already had his supper, and I decide to humour him. A grown man knows his own stomach. And, even if our fishing lines will stay empty for the rest of the dark season, we won't starve. The villagers will take care of us: they've always kept their side of the bargain. I glance along the dark walls, at the rows of shelves and hooks with jars and bundles neatly stacked and regularly turned and dusted. My father keeps a clean house – indeed, I've heard them joke in the village that the only thing he ever needed a wife was for bearing me. And I believe they're right.

I don't remember my mother at all. As long as my memory stretches, it's always been my father and myself, taking care of each other. And of the village. Father says that as long as the lore goes, there has always been a Lamplighter living in this cottage. The skill has been passed down generations, usually from father to son. The Lamplighter's task is a straightforward one, and yet something that cannot be taught to an outsider. When I was born, my father knew immediately that I would take over his post one day. He stopped wishing for a son – and started neglecting his wife so that finally she gave up and died. Or that's what I've heard the villagers say.

Although my father has been the Lamplighter for forty years or more, he has taught me nothing. Everything I know about light and dark, the caprices of weather and the changing seasons I've either known all my life, or picked up through careful observation. Ever since

I could keep up with him, father has taken me on longer and longer trips on the ice; together we've watched one winter after another arrive, endure, and finally give up under the growing light of the sun.

Now father is saying that I have all the skill it takes to guide the village to the other side of winter.

'What happens if I fail?' I asked him once. 'Will the sun refuse to come back?'

A vague gesture. 'It's not about that. The seasons turn regardless of our efforts. It's about the people: what they need, and what they think they need.'

'So you're saying it makes no difference what we do.'

'That's not what I'm saying at all. It makes all the difference in the world. A Lamplighter is like the baker. Anyone can make their own bread, and yet we prefer this one person in the village to get up early each morning and sweat at the oven for us. Anyone can walk the winter ice; anyone can raise a lantern to hold back the darkness – and yet most people never will.'

'But there's the promise as well,' I remind him.

'Yes. The village gave us shelter, in return of our skill. We track the light, count the hours, keep the lamps lit – and they tolerate us.'

For we, even after centuries of service, are still outsiders. Anyone who marries into the Lamplighter's family will have to forsake her own. I think my father, in ignoring his wife, made the only right choice: as his firstborn, I'm tolerated here. Any other children would have faced a cruel isolation; having no remarkable skill, they would have had to live out their lives helping their parents – and, finally, me. The one talent that gives reassurance to the village is also seen as an unnatural taint – useful, but ultimately dangerous.

After I've eaten, we talk about my day. Father asks the usual questions – about my route, the traps I checked and the tracks I saw, and what the weather was like farther on the ice. How many lanterns had burned out by the time I got back, and how much oil remains in the container. I've fixed these things in my memory while walking, so as to remember even the tiniest of details. I want to prolong this firelit moment, the flicker of the dying flames in the hearth, the soft popping of sparks. Our only safeguard against the pervasive darkness.

But then we know the essence of night, my father and I. Unlike the villagers, we don't waste oil or candles for such simple tasks as eating. The lore says that the Lamplighters carry a bright flame within them, at all times, and that they are immune to the perils of the outside world. I've heard the villagers say that our dreams are of the day, and therefore we're not afraid to close our eyes against the approaching night.

I don't know what other people dream of, in their bright bedchambers, under the oppressive eiderdown. I've heard my father whimpering in his sleep, but haven't dared to ask him what he sees. My own dreams are mainly of ice and rock – of cold things and hard things. Things that have no yearnings. Yet, there are nights when I cannot sleep for the scorching flame inside me.

The day begins at sunrise. In winter, when the working hours are few, there's a feverish bustle in the streets from the earliest dawn to the falling of dusk. I'm often awakened by the sound of clanging metal or breaking ice, or else to the shrieks of children who chase each other out of doors, burning pent-up energy. Father is always up before me, swearing at the stove or at his damp socks. Neither of us are creatures of the first light; inner light or no, it takes some time to get us reconciled to the new day.

There's usually something fresh for breakfast: a piping-hot loaf, a liver pie, or silver-sided fish straight from the sea. Morning is the best time, food-wise. Father says that's because the folk still remember the terror of the night before, and are more apt to remember us as well. It used to worry me that some day the villagers might forget about us altogether, or that they would find someone else to banish the night for them. Neither of us are well adapted to the endless requirements of domestic life: father would rather go about shirtless than to pick up a darning needle; I have no idea how to milk a goat or grow a turnip. Whatever we need, our neighbours are happy to provide.

Lately a new kind of fear has begun to haunt me. I'm not afraid of the fickleness of folk anymore; I know that ours is a rare breed and the chances of another one wandering into the village are remote. Father seems sure of my gift: otherwise he would never send me out into the darkness alone. I, on the other hand, am not so sure anymore. Some days I walk and walk along the familiar routes, and cannot remember what I'm supposed to be looking for. I stand there, listening to the wind howling against the ice, and slowly begin to lose my grip. I long to be blown apart, to be mingled with the white oblivion of the longest season, just to feel some other essence against mine.

Yesterday I heard voices on the wind. Human or animal I couldn't tell, but my first impulse was to run towards them. Not with a harpoon in hand, but open-armed and curious. This of course is the first sign of mid-winter madness. Nothing good ever comes from the outside, I've been told: all who speak a different tongue or wear a different cut of clothes should be shunned, if not shot on sight. Although the villagers take care of each other readily, all possessions are jealously guarded against intruders; in this harsh world there just isn't enough to go round. Yet to me it seems that the light and warmth of a fireplace can be shared with a dozen people, just as easily as with two.

I think father agrees. I'd like to ask him, but lately he's begun to turn inwards. He studies his face in the darkness of a window as if he doesn't recognise his own reflection. Some days he calls me by my mother's name. The worst days are those when he refuses to get out of bed and just stares at the ceiling, unhearing and unspeaking. After a day like that, the only thing I can do is to walk as far as I can, and lean towards the foreign voices on the ice.

For three weeks now I've come home empty-handed. The villagers go on with their lives behind their shut doors at night, hoping that the blizzards will sweep the winter away in their wake. They'll be needing a sign soon. Something that says it's safe to walk abroad again; that there's no need to fear the winter night that chills the blood in their veins and brings unseen dangers to their doorstep. That the seals and whales are coming for the brief season of breeding and bloodshed. I should be looking for that sign, scouring the ice-covered vastness for it – on my hands and knees if necessary. At night, I should be questing out with my mind, or dreaming of bright things to come.

But that's not what I do. Each day takes me farther from the village, away from the complacent circle of the island. I walk in a straight line until I'm exhausted, hoping for the darkness to overtake me. Yet every time I turn back before the light fails, and find my way unerringly home. Like a bird returning I have my compass set for life.

Today, as I make my way south, I see the dark shapes of swans on the horizon: the first migrants are on their way to their summer homes. Somewhere, the ice has started to melt; cracks are appearing in the uniform surface. Soon, the bridge that connects us with the dangers of the outside world will be broken, and the village be safe again for the warm, light months. During the summer, the sea currents will lead astray anyone who tries to navigate north.

I know then what I must do. It must be soon: the nights are still cold enough, and spring always has a few storms in store. On foot, it'll take me days to get to the next island. The half-remembered wisdom of our people says that even by boat the way is long and difficult. This is of course why they chose our island in the first place. No one gets here, and no one leaves. The people living here see the first light of the coming summer: they have the guidance of the Lamplighter and the long lore that goes with it.

The swans are a sign enough, whether I'll be here to report their return or no. The sun will make its inevitable circuit; birds and seals will find their nesting-places and grass will push its way out of the warming earth. If the villagers want reassurance, they'll have to venture out to the ice to look for it themselves. If they want light, they'll have to learn to keep their own lamps burning.

At night, as soon father has fallen asleep, I start packing a small bag. I don't have a lot of possessions to begin with, and I don't really know what I'll need on my journey or after it. I'd like to take some of this familiar darkness with me; I'd like to take the soft sound of my father breathing. He told me today he won't live to see the summer. I think he knows my plans, and approves. He knows that even a fast promise of five hundred years' standing has to be broken someday.

Father says that a Lamplighter only sees a small way ahead, but within his circle of light everything is safe and certain. The flame I carry grows brighter by the day; I fear that if I keep it trapped, it will eventually burn me alive.

Anne Karppinen

Anne Karppinen is *a university teacher, translator and musician. In addition to a PhD in Contemporary Culture, she holds an M.A. in English, and did Creative Writing in the UK as a part of her studies. Her short story 'You're All the Same to Me' recently appeared in Tales from the Moonlit Path; her book, The Songs of Joni Mitchell, was published by Routledge in 2016.*

Fixed Line
Denali Stannard

Fixed Line

The radio coughed out dead air and a voice that said, "Lost him. Going back for- Lost. Can't feel- Lost. Lost."

It had been saying that for the past half an hour, and Cal nudged the frequency a little to make it stop. It was nothing she wasn't used to, but she was tightly wound, alone in the tent, with only the dull thud of ropes slapping nylon to keep her company.

It couldn't hurt to check in, even though the party was likely well out of range and they hadn't responded to her for over an hour.

"Buster crew, this is Dr. Bridges from Camp Three. Checking in on your status, over."

Static but no voices; not Iumo's deep rumble or Rio's sharp cackle. Cal tried again, willing the transmission up the icefall, through the maze of crevasses and frayed rope.

"Busters, this is Bridges. It's just me and the ghost in the machine down here, you gotta give me something. Maybe a pity laugh for the joke?" Cal discovered she was laughing herself, a little hysterically. Not a good look on a public frequency. "Um. Over."

"Over," said the radio, a man's voice.

Cal's thumb turned white as she jabbed it down on the push-to-talk button. "Iumo?"

"Over," said the radio, thin and childlike now. "Over? Over! Over!" There was a chorus of voices, singing, moaning, screaming. There was the crash of ice and the groan of wind, and the crowding voices of the dead.

Cal left the radio in the corner and burrowed into her sleeping bag, trying to ignore the tapping against the tent walls; trying not to picture fingers, black-tipped, burnt with cold.

If the party up on the serac had anything to say about it, the voices would be gone come dawn.

That's why you hired exorcists, after all.

The corpses had been piling up on Neverfall for years. There were slopes and ridges where the snow was dotted with the parkas and down suits of the dead. Someone should do something, said opinion pieces and families who bridled at their loved ones reduced to macabre landmarks. 'Turn left at the skeleton in the yellow jacket taking a breather against a rock. That's Sharit Walker, his kids were in the papers the other week, begging for someone to bring him home.'

But the mountain kept what you gave her, and there was no chipping a body free of half a ton of ice and shale, then carrying the frozen weight of it to basecamp. Not when it was five miles down in air so thin you might as well be breathing vacuum, ribs cracked from your coughing and your blood thick as slurry.

And if the bodies were bad, the ghosts were worse.

They flapped in the wind, bright and ragged as prayer flags. Scraps of Gore-Tex and leather hung on frames of bone and memory; faces swollen, frost-scared blurs. Sometimes they stayed where they died, wailing and babbling, replaying their final gasping moments. Sometimes they followed climbers from base camp to summit, or clustered around pitched tents, pressing against the fly.

It was horrible. It was a safety hazard. Their whisperings choked the airwaves, making it harder and harder to tell the frantic call of an injured climber from the echoes of an accident of thirty years before.

"It's the responsible thing to do," Rio had said when the papers asked her why she was spearheading the Neverfall Cleansing Campaign.

Responsibility nothing. Rio Varga had the same instinct for publicity that cats had for mice, the same habit of leaving torn up press clippings on their bed. Rio climbed like a cat too, lithe and graceful, leaping from hold to precarious hold, teeth and tawny hair flashing in sunlight unfiltered by atmosphere.

Rio had drummed up thousands of dollars in supplies and sponsorships, and two of the valley's fittest exorcists swathed in prayer beads and down jackets. And now here they were, on an expedition to the peak of the tallest mountain in the world.

Here Cal was, waking in the dark to the radio popping and whispering.

"Cal," came Rio's voice, in the snow-soft murmur she saved for when it was just them. "Where are you? *Cal.*"

That was all that came through. Cal threw herself from her sleeping bag and sat freezing in her thermal underwear trying to get her back.

By morning, the radio was still dead. It hadn't said another word - not in Rio's voice, not in Iumo's, not in anyone's - and that scared Cal more than any choir of ghosts.

The team was supposed to check in when they made it to alpine Camp Four. They were supposed to make it there by 1700. By 0400, they still hadn't checked in.

And Dr. Cal Bridges had hit her limit.

"I've been up there before," Cal told the blue-cloaked skybride. The woman was a devotee of Neverfall, the mountain climbers nicknamed the Bride and courted just as fervently. Blasphemously, if you minded what the skybrides said about the sanctity of the mountain goddess's snow.

Cal didn't ask what this priestess was doing at Camp Three, or mention that on her last attempt Cal had turned back two hundred meters from the summit. "And the Pike last year. I know what I'm doing. I won't slow you down."

The priestess looked doubtful. When you were twitchy, bespectacled, and ninety pounds in your crampons, people made assumptions about your climbing ability, but at least this woman looked like she'd hold Cal in equally low regard if she was six two and built like a linebacker.

"We want the same thing. It makes sense to pool resources."

"I want you the fuck off this mountain," said the priestess. She was half a foot taller than Cal, imposing in a blue snowsuit and iron spiked boots.

"I'm sorry?"

"I want you off my mountain," she repeated. "You, your friends, their bodies, their ghosts. I want your garbage gone, your shit scoured from my lady's flanks. I want all of you, living or dead, off my *fucking* mountain."

Cal remembered suddenly why this woman looked so familiar; she'd been the spokesperson during the May season, two years ago, when a whole expedition had gone missing.

"We told them not to come here," she'd told reporters who'd come looking for rustic prayers for lost souls. "*Everything* told them not to come here, from the blood thickening in their veins to the rising waters in their lungs. Stop sending your fools here to die. We can't hear ourselves think for their babble in the night."

There had been a stink about it. Reams of commentary on the bitter locals who hadn't turned enough profit on the ascension industry and resented the success of those who had. Rio had read it to Cal over breakfast.

"Okay," said Cal, hooking her mittened thumbs into her pack straps and staring up at the woman who carried an ice axe like a crozier and disdain like a miter. "Fair enough. But I'm not turning back. My crew is up there. My friends, my -" Not her girlfriend, not after the night at Camp Two, with the thrown cook pot, with Cal's furious tears and Rio's exasperated shouts. "-my friends are up there." Her *only* friends, because Cal didn't make friends easily, and the ones she had were the crazies who threw themselves at the roof of the sky to see if they'd stick. Her friends were big Iumo, whose family talked about him as if he were already dead, and the Laskor twins, who had short-roped each other up Hiluae'a and lost four fingers between them; and yes, Rio, who had broken Cal's heart a dozen times over and who Cal was not about to let vanish without answering for it. "There's a crew up there freezing on the col, and if we let them die, it will be half a dozen new ghosts keeping you up."

"Half a dozen and one," the priestess muttered, breaking eye contact to look Cal up and down. "Fine. Let's go."

It came as an honest shock. Cal had been asking around all morning and everyone she'd approached had pointed to the storm that'd rolled in the night before and was looking to come back around. They'd pointed out that Rio's group were likely safe at Camp Four and hadn't called it in, so going up after them was pointless. Or else they hadn't made it to camp, and going after them was even more pointless.

The woman was already walking away, through the tents of Camp Three towards the ice face that was their pathway to the heights. Her strides were long and Cal hurried to keep pace. The priestess walked like a boulder tumbled, like her arrival was utterly inevitable and her goddess help anyone that tried to stop it. "Let me know when you're ready," the priestess said, spinning open a carabiner at her waist.

"What should I call you?" asked Cal. Being roped to the woman impressed upon her, like it hadn't before, that it was the two of them against the mountain and its secrets; the skybride her only defense against a fall from the heights. "I can't go up on a rope by someone whose name I don't know."

"Anja," said the skybride, and anchored Cal for her climb.

Cal had brought the handheld radio with her and she flicked it on and off as they picked their way up the icefall. Around them, seracs groaned and sweated in the sun, sparkling like the fanciful ramparts of a glass castle.

The first ghost was waiting at the top.

It was an old one, in wool and leather. As Cal flexed her fingers in their gloves and stamped her feet to keep warm, it shuffled closer and closer. By the time Anja hauled herself onto the ledge, huffing in huge lungfuls of meager air, it was almost pressed against Cal's side, stinking of mildew and meat shriveling in the sun.

"Help." Its voice was wind whistling through rocks. "Help. Help me. Help."

Cal tilted her body away from the shadowy bone and sinew, like she did with creeps on the train in the city. "Anja. Can you help it? Please?"

Hunched over, arms braced against her legs, Anja grinned between pants for breath. "Exorcise it? Easily."

"Because," And this had been bothering her for a while. "If you *can*, why haven't you done it before?"

"You and Varga spoke to our Reverend Mother, didn't you?" Anja's raised eyebrow said that she knew that they had, and knew exactly what the Reverend Mother had said; something similar to Anja, minus the cussing. "Evey climber hurts her, even us. You can climb fast and take smoke baths and mouth the right prayers, but a trespass is a trespass. Pain is pain, however sorry you are for causing it."

"But you're up here." Up here with a fall of two hundred feet behind them and something fifty years dead at their side.

"You're a doctor." Anja gestured at Cal and the tattoos on the backs of her hands, under her gloves, that mapped out her profession. "You know that cutting out a tumor means pain. Sometimes the end justifies the means. The Reverend Mother doesn't think so. I do."

Cal had amputated too many gangrenous, black-nailed fingers and toes to disagree. "So you're a heretic?"

"No. I just don't have the patience for bitching and moaning when there's something I can *do*. Speaking of - " She clasped her mitten in her teeth and drew it off, then went rummaging in another pocket for yak knucklebones strung on a thong and a sprig of something resinous. "Set this on fire, would you?"

The flames, when they caught, threw up a fitful plume of smoke, snatched into ribbons by the wind. Cal hunkered over, shielding it as Anja rattled the knucklebones and straightened up to her full height.

This high, the magic caught easier than the fire had. Cal had seen enough exorcisms at the hospital that they'd become as mundane as sending biowaste to the incinerator, but here there was no slow leech of light and life as the spell took hold. The world tipped from color to the charcoal daubs of the Other Place so quickly that Cal almost dropped the sprig, wheezing like she'd been punched.

There was no mountain here, only a black plain beneath a midnight sky. Anja was as solid as ever, the shadows sliding across her round, indifferent face. Before them was the ghost, wrapped in frayed ropes and the ragged remains of a face.

"Help," it said.

"That's why we're here," said Anja, surprisingly soft. "Tell us what happened."

Deaths at the hospital were usually easy. Old or sick or both, with time enough to make some kind of peace before the end. The ones that died beneath the scalpel on operating tables, or came in mangled from accidents and past the point of saving, those needed the coaxing of a priest.

But the ghosts of Neverfall were another matter. You didn't climb her if you didn't want it so badly that you were willing to die for it. And that, ironically enough, made for ghosts that couldn't accept it.

"Help?" said the ghost again.

"We're here to help," said Anja. "Tell me what went wrong."

The ghost was only shadow and despair, so it caught Cal off guard when it said, quite clearly, "Djeri went ahead, when the storm came up. Whiteout."

Cal recognized the cadence of a climbing tale; like any one of her friends telling the story of that one bad spring, that gulch with the bad snow, that time Billie nearly lost an eye in the backcountry.

She hunkered down on her heels like she did when listening to a good disaster, training her ear to the part of the story where she could say *'there's* where it went wrong' and avoid repeating it herself one day. "Were you roped together?"

"Whiteout," repeated the ghost. Ragged hands waved at the torn ropes encircling it. This place, on the other side of death, was mutable in the way the world was not. As the ghost spoke, fat white flakes began to fall, soft and textureless as ash. Faster and faster, piling around their ankles until Cal could barely see Anja beside her, and the ghost was only a silhouette against the storm. "I was moving too slow. Lungs. *Hurt.*" It let out a keening noise. "I can't keep up, wait up - I'm going to take a breather, let me take a rest… I'm running low… Djeri, I can't see you… Help, help, help…" It dissolved into wails again, swaying where it stood.

"What's your name, bud?" Cal had helped countless raving climbers, delirious with cold and infection and fluid in the brain. She'd held the hands of a hundred frightened patients so deep in shock they couldn't tell her where the bullet had gone in.

It was amazing how a name could anchor you in all that pain. Sometimes it was the only thing you could hold onto.

"You're not alone," Anja added. "We'll help you down. What's your name, honey?"

The whisper floated on the cold air. Cal held it in her mind, and Anja caught it on her knucklebones and held it to the flame.

She spoke the name into the flickering heat and held out her hand. The ghost moved towards her, a shadow reaching -

When its fingertips met the flame, it sighed. And was gone.

Anja blew out the herbs. As the scent faded and the smoke blew away, they were back on the mountainside. There was ash on the ground, and an old, frayed rope.

"Rest in peace," said Cal, inadequately.

"Remain there," said Anja, and beckoned Cal up the crag.

One down, several hundred to go.

The storm came from nowhere.

"Don't you pass out on me," Anja warned. "I'm not saying I couldn't carry you-"

"My twelve-year-old niece can carry me," Cal mumbled. And she had, one time when Cal was babysitting and Ruby had gotten annoyed with her strictures on screen time.

"I have no interest in hauling a flatlander's ass down my lady's flanks, you hear? If you faint, you're still responsible for getting your jackrabbit butt back to base." As Anja chided, her hand was on the small of Cal's back, bracing her against the wind. The security of it allowed Cal to take a few steps. She leaned forward, braced her weight on her ice axe, and somehow found her rhythm again.

Anja's hand patted her lightly between the shoulder blades and then was gone.

Rio's hands had been large and strong too, but always cold. She'd hefted Cal up more cliff faces than Cal could count; braced her on snow bridges until she found her balance; reached out in the dark of their tent to cup Cal's face in a calloused palm. The skin of her fingertips was always rough, her skin dry and cool. She could pull up her own body weight on nothing more than those fingertips, tipping herself up rock faces on the sea stacks back home. She could pull Cal to her, too, and did.

But there was no touch now, cold or otherwise.

Cal turned her face into the wind and let it freeze her tears. The world narrowed to the snow beneath her feet, the rise and fall of her ice-clotted boots and the ache in her lungs.

She almost stumbled into Anja's back. And then, staggering past, almost stumbled over the body slumped on the trail.

There weren't any known dead on this ridge, and for a moment Cal panicked, wondering how far they'd gone off course. But then it stirred.

It was Iumo, face down upon the ice.

Anja was already on her knees, rolling him over. There was an overhang ten feet away, and if they could get him into its shelter it might save him. But Iumo was a big man and up here ten feet might as well be ten miles. Anja strained, grabbing under his armpits and heaving until the veins stood out upon her temples. He slid about a foot.

"He'll have to walk," Cal said, crouching. "Iumo! Hey, buddy, what are you doing lying around up here?" Behind his frosted-over goggles, Iumo's eyelids fluttered. His pulse was weak and very slow and one of his gloves was off, half-buried beside him. Too late, almost certainly, but she eased it back onto his hand, over fingers cold and stiff as chicken straight from the freezer. Frostbite was a problem for if he survived. "*Iumo*, wake up. I've got a skybride here, don't go cluttering up her mountain right in front of her."

Iumo blinked again and his dark eyes focused on her face. Iumo, who'd helped her move into her last apartment, who came to her for advice on asking out the cute girl at the library, and who, after her last fight with Rio, had dropped a heavy hand on her shoulder and said there was no shame in walking away. His lips formed her name without sound and Cal smiled encouragingly. It would be easy to panic, but she'd been doing this a long time. She was almost as practiced at losing friends as she was at saving lives.

"Cal?" he said, slurring the name.

"That's right. Come on, we can't drag your ass so you're gonna have to walk." He had half a tank of oxygen left, though the valve had frozen over. She pounded it free, turned the gas on a notch and strapped the mask in place. "Breathe, Iumo. Let's walk."

With her and Anja's help - mostly Anja's - they got him upright and staggering the ten feet into the cave. They wrapped him in a bag while Anja poured a thermos of syrupy tea down his throat and Cal radioed for help.

"They're sending two traversairs up for you," Cal told him, relieved to see he was starting to shiver. "What the hell happened up there? Why didn't you make it to Camp Four?"

"HAPE," Iumo said. His teeth clacked, and Cal's heart sank. High altitude pulmonary edema was the mountain's favorite killer. "It got one of the exorcist kids. Rio went up with Hachi and the other one, while Hani and I tried to get her down to Camp Three. Then the storm blew in. Lost them in it."

"Rio went up?" Acid seared Cal's stomach; fear, but also anger. "She left you?"

"Gotta finish the job," mumbled Iumo. "Left us with an extra canister of O₂. Hers. Said she'd summited before without gas, so it was no big."

Cal sat back on her heels, fighting panic. Yes, Rio had climbed twice and summited once without oxygen. But less oxygen meant you moved and thought slower, and delusions grew fast. A wise climber would never guide without it, not when other lives depended on the decisions you made and the steps you cut. But of course Rio had given hers up for a sick ghostbuster. Of course she had.

Cal urged Iumo to take another gulp of tea. "Drink it all. How long ago did you lose Hani?"

He shuddered again and Cal was glad; at least his body was responding to the cold rather than succumbing to it. "Aren't he… with you?"

"No, bud," said Cal, gently as she was able. "I just found you, remember? You're the one who told me you lost him."

"We need to bring him lower," said Anja. She was watching Iumo's eyes and the stiffness of his movements. "Wait much longer and he won't be able to move under his own steam. Got to get him to thicker air, closer to the traversairs."

"Okay," said Cal, but as Anja clipped herself to Iumo's harness to short rope him down the step, she hesitated in the alcove. Was that a cry on the wind?

"It's probably-" Anja called, but Cal ignored her, even though Anja was probably right.

The voice was not of someone living.

Cal hadn't realized how high they'd made it; up to the ridge that climbers called the Maidenhead. It was marked by a rough heap of rocks piled over a long-dead climber on the side of the trail. The cairn hadn't held up against years of howling weather, and scraps of fabric peeked between icy gaps; through one, a shredded glove revealed a single white finger.

The ghost it belonged to stood on the ridge and wept.

Cal took no notice because huddled beside the cairn were two figures, heads bowed.

One was Hani, chin tucked to his chest, the scarf his husband had sent with him still wrapped around his throat. He was holding a smaller figure, the scrappy acolyte girl from the monastery, the one who could hang by her toes and had bragged about the demons she'd banished.

The ice was inches thick on their faces.

Cal let out a sob and slumped to her knees. The girl - Jaine, Cal remembered - had her fingers wrapped around amber prayer beads. There was a burnt twig in the alcove behind her knees. Her nose had already turned black, and her eyes were open, pupils fixed and dilated. She couldn't have been more than eighteen.

Hani was braced behind the girl, his shoulders hunched like he was trying to fold around her. Despite the thick hoar of frost, wisps of his hair had escaped his hood and were blowing, gingery and ragged, around his face. Choking, Cal reached out, cupping a mittened hand around his pale cheek, unable to bear leaving him frozen over like a portrait behind glass. She chipped at the ice, knowing the memory of his face would haunt her worse than any ghost; knowing too that she would memorize it even if it killed her. It was the least she could do for his husband when she brought the news.

The ice around his lips splintered. A puff of mist rose on the air before being whipped away on the wind and Cal gasped. She could see Hani's eyes now.

He blinked.

The plan had been to make it back to Camp Three, stabilize Iumo and Hani, radio down to base for a helicopter, then turn around and head back up for Rio and the others. An expedition bound folk closer than any blood tie, and Cal should know; of her four siblings, she was only on speaking terms with one. Hachi and Hani had been the ones to bring her champagne when she got her residency assignment. Tasi, the tall exorcist with the braids who'd only known Cal a week, had held her feet against her bare stomach to warm them one night at Base when Cal had forgotten her boot warmers.

You didn't leave family behind, and yet that was exactly what Cal did.

She sat in the tent the traversairs had erected, listened to the wind scream, and only barely restrained herself from screaming back. The storm had worsened as soon as they'd made it to camp, their O2 was dangerously low and they would need a resupply from another team hiking up to meet them before they could ascend. Cal wasn't Search and Rescue. She was the expedition's doctor, and the place she was needed was where there were patients.

There was plenty to do. There was the lukewarm water she was carefully working over Iumo's hands, and the hyperbaric chamber Hani had been in for the last hour. There were injections to administer to counteract the edema in their lungs, and she couldn't hide her relief when Hani twitched and Iumo cursed her out for jabbing it into their hips. "This probably means you won't lose your ass."

"Tragedy prevented," murmured Iumo, and she started to pat dry his hands so that she could bandage them.

It was only once both he and Hani had sunk into a fitful doze that Cal let herself despair.

She sat in the corner, head in her hands, sleeping bag around her shoulders, and let the tears drip onto the polyester. Anja was outside, talking to the traversairs, and Cal knew she was fatigued from the exorcism and the arduous trip down; knew that she should go out and shout the woman into at least an hour of sleep.

Instead, Cal flicked her radio on and off the way Anja thumbed her prayer beads, and listened to the static.

"Cal?" said the radio. A snow-soft whisper, warm and intimate as a hand on her shoulder.

"*Rio.*" Cal rose to her knees, sleeping bag slipping, thumb jabbing the radio. "Rio! Can you hear me?"

Static. Was that a whisper? She could swear Rio was on the other side of the tent wall, that she'd spoken right into Cal's ear.

"Sorry," said Anja outside the tent flap. "Sorry, I was - Wanted to check in on how the boys are doing. Sorry, that was me."

But Cal would know the difference between Rio's whisper and Anja's even if there were only two molecules of oxygen left in the world, and she surged out of the tent, slipping as her boot liners hit the packed snow.

"I heard her." She spun wildly on her heel and over-balanced. Only Anja's grasp at her elbow kept her from hitting the snow chin first and Cal bit her tongue as she was jerked upright. "I heard her, she's-"

Cal cast her eyes about frantically, as if the swirling snow and implacable headwalls around them offered any answers. Anja glanced around too, uneasy. Their gazes found the northwest corner of camp at the same time, and Anja's hand went tight on Cal's arm.

There was a figure there, wind tossing its sandy hair. Red mittens, red boots, a black snowsuit. A mouth, opened in an anguished cry.

It wore Rio's clothes, but it had no face.

"Rio!" Cal screamed, but no sound came out.

Anja's arm was tight around her waist, holding her back, but Cal pulled away with animal strength, her feet skidding on the ice. She threw herself towards Rio, answering the wail with a wail of her own, and it was only when Anja brought her down that she stopped moving, stopped fighting.

The figure was gone.

She was feet from where it had been. Had she reached it, she would have been balanced on a black ice precipice, beyond which the cwm dropped away a thousand feet or more.

"It was Rio," rasped Cal, blood leaking from her mouth.

"It was a ghost," said Anja, very gently for someone lying with all her weight on Cal's back.

They were both right.

The knowledge of it threw Cal reeling into an agony too savage to endure, and she was unconscious before her head hit the snow.

Her dreams were all of Rio.

Not of that cold, dead, scratching thing pulling itself out of a crevasse, stumbling on broken legs, mouth yawning open onto nothing.

She dreamed of their apartment, tiny and sun-littered, thirty minutes from the hospital, ten from the climbing gym, with the pullup bar installed in the bedroom door frame. Rio would never walk under it without doing a set. She'd never walk past Cal without kissing the top of her head and sliding a hand into Cal's back pocket. Rio's hands with their split nails and calluses, Rio's cackling jaybird laugh and the way she threw her whole body into it like a dive, Rio's mouth, always quirking up at the corners.

"Cal," Rio whispered, in the soft voice she saved for regrets. She'd used it when Cal screamed at her about the cheating. She hadn't when Cal begged her not to climb before the storm because the only other woman in Rio's life that mattered was her Bride. "Hey, Cal, hey baby. It wasn't your fault. You're my anchor, girl. My fixed line. You know I'll always come back to you."

Cal woke to the taste of blood in her mouth, a cough in her chest, and a bleary, high-altitude headache. Also to snoring, and the heat of another body pressed against hers. Anja smelled as bad as Cal probably did, but there was an animal comfort in the closeness of another body and she didn't move away.

Freeing her hand from the sleeping bag so she could check her watch woke Anja, who snorted, rolled over and explained gruffly, "You were shivering by the time I got you in here. And I didn't trust you not to wake up and go throw yourself off the cwm."

"Thanks," Cal said, not especially grateful. The drop would have been easier. Or staying in this sleeping bag forever. But she had to get up, step into the cold, check on her surviving friends, climb a mountain no one ought to climb, and follow a ghost. Her ex-girlfriend and now ex-everything else.

The dim light of a solar lantern flattened Anja's face into a mask. The mountain had weathered her plain features even plainer, and under a short cap of lusterless black hair, her eyes were as black as her mountain's rock, sharp and unyielding, set deep in her face. Her mouth, though, was surprisingly soft. "You loved her."

Past tense. Cal ducked her head, breaking eye contact in case she started crying. "The last thing I said to her was- it wasn't even, 'I hate you,' or 'I never want to see you again.' I said, 'I fucking hate your mom's cooking'. And if we hadn't had that stupid fight…" If Cal had climbed with her, instead of sulking back in camp, then Cal could have told her to turn back sooner, told her to keep her oxygen and stop being a dumbass-

"The storm wouldn't have blown in?" Anja asked, implacable.

Cal shifted so her whole face was pressed to Anja's shoulder and her voice came out muffled, barely audible. "Let me wallow."

"You're too sensible for that."

"You don't know me."

"Pssh." Anja's hand slid away, back into the bag before the cold stole all the warmth from it. "Varga I understand, and those boys defrosting in the other tent. But what the hell are *you* doing this for?"

There were a thousand answers to that. Cal had always said, 'Because someone has to be designated driver,' when people asked, so that Rio would laugh and clap her shoulder.

You courted the Bride because some part of you wanted her more than you feared the fall, and that was something Cal had understood since med school. Since she'd stitched close a gash gouged by a climber's rebounding ice axe and Rio had grinned at her with bloody teeth and asked what she was doing later. "Why did you become a priest?"

"I was a guide for a while, until I saw what it was doing to the mountain. Saw what it was doing to the people." Cal could feel the weight of her gaze like a physical touch. "But the truth is I *missed* this. I know how much Neverfall's hurting, I can feel the pain grow like a tumor every meter we go up. I got myself convinced that coming up here, easing her as much as I could, was the right thing to do, but part of me jumped at the excuse."

"You've freed three ghosts and prevented three more." Cal remembered Anja's gentleness with the ghost in the whiteout. Her concern for Iumo and Hani. Her warm chest pressed against Cal's back. "I think you're doing this for the right reasons. Listen, I'm going back up as soon as the wind lifts, but you don't have to come. It was selfish to make you do this much."

Anja grunted and, looking up, Cal saw lantern light reflected in the black depths of her eyes. "If we find people, you aren't getting them down alone. If we find ghosts, well, that's why I'm up here. Might as well make it count."

Because the mountain had a cruel sense of humor, the morning dawned clear and beautiful.

It was a perfect day for summiting and groups were already setting out for the top, laden with warm clothes and fresh oxygen and everything that could have kept Rio alive had she encountered it soon enough. Cal wondered if the group ahead would find the bodies first, or if Rio and Tasi and Hachi were scattered to the four directions, tossed from the step or buried beneath blown snow. It could be years before their bones were revealed.

In the long night of her grief, Cal had tamped the loss down until it was like the numbness in her toes, pressed to the front of her boots. She knew that if she pressed too hard the pain would come, but for now, she could stumble forward, moving only a little more stiffly than usual. Once she descended to the valley she would stretch her feet to the fire and let the pain rise through her.

But here and now there was only air for one obsession at a time.

"The thing is," said Cal, and stopped. Anja looked up.

The thing was that they might never find Rio's body, or Hachi's, or the girl. They might never find their spirits, either - Ghosts crowded the slopes, but without the minds that had once contained them they were nothing but those last impressions of life. Nothing but panic and confusion and regret, and sometimes that drove them into tents and through radio frequencies, and sometimes they stayed in their ravines, waiting for others to join them. Sometimes they lay under the snow, whispering. Sometimes they blew away on the wind. They didn't come to you when you sought them.

There were *hundreds* of them.

She and Anja could never get rid of them all, not the way they had been doing it. Not one by one in painstaking ritual, finding their names, accepting their grief, showing them the way out. It would be a gargantuan undertaking. It would drive them mad long before they made a dent in the spectral mass.

They'd been fools to think this could work.

"The thing is," said Cal, "that Rio would never leave the mountain." When she saw Anja's mouth open, she went on to curtail her. "She wasn't a holy woman, not literally wed to it like you, but she might as *well* have been. She dreamed of it every night, talked about it every minute. She failed the summit four times before she managed it, and each time I asked if she was done, she looked at me like I was crazy. Was she done with the mountain? It wasn't done with *her*. It was like how some people are with drink, or how some people are with -"

"Lovers," said Anja.

"Yes," said Cal. "Even if we found - her body," her voice caught and cracked, "her spirit wouldn't leave. Her spirit wants the mountain. And Sister, she's not the only one."

Anja sat back and squinted up towards the peak, where the snow and mist streamed out like a veil.

"Climbers ain't regular souls," said Cal, quoting Iumo's favorite saying. "They're going to be hard to shake from your lady."

"Good I'm not a jealous lover." Anja put her hands in her armpits and huffed out a breath. "So. What then? If my bones and herbs and beads aren't enough for your dead climbers, what is? What do you propose, Dr. Bridges?"

"A relationship takes two," said Dr. Bridges, watching the veil break apart in morning winds, "And so does a breakup."

They climbed in silence.

With every crunch of her crampons, Cal expected to see Rio. A corpse or a ghost or Rio alive and coughing blood and lymph, or laughing and telling her to hurry.

Hani hadn't said anything about Hachi when Cal checked in before beginning the climb - still too spaced out by the cold, the thin air, and what she hoped wasn't brain damage. Iumo knew they weren't looking for the living any longer, but had only clapped her shoulder with his good hand and said he hoped Mama Mountain gave them a break.

She did. The weather held.

"To the summit?" Cal had asked, and Anja had shaken her head.

"It'll work better lower, and not only because we'll have more chance of being alive for it. Up past the Maidenhead, where the ground levels. As long as we're into the death zone, that should be high enough."

A part of Cal wanted to argue. Wanted to be sure it worked. Wanted to summit. She choked it back like bile and focused on keeping her fingers nimble and her respirator clear of ice.

She slipped once, foot sliding free of its hold, and for a moment and the fear rose in her stomach as she dropped, only to be brought up short with the clank of her ascender catching and a bruising jolt from her harness. Above her on the ropes, Anja peered down and Cal, panting into her mask, shot her a quick thumbs up.

After yesterday's climb, this was almost relaxing. The worst had happened. It was already too late. Death was immutable.

But the world beyond was not. Up on the Maidenhead, above the cairn where they'd found Hani and left poor Jaine beneath another mound of stones, Anja pressed her palms together, beads wrapped loose around her wrists.

Up here, the spell caught even quicker than it had before. The world went black and soundless almost before the flames caught Anja's herbs. The midnight plane wavered like a mirage, and Anja grunted with effort.

Magic had never been Cal's forte, but Anja had talked her through the basics. Magic was wanting things, and one thing Rio had taught Cal was how to want.

Cal wanted the mountain. Rio's conquest, Anja's bride, with her veil of glittering ice, Neverfall in all her majesty and treachery. There were lovelier mountains, more technical climbs, but they paled to Neverfall, whose weight distorted the world around her, drew priests and climbers and nobodies with something to prove. She collected ghosts like notches on the bedpost.

They no longer stood upon a black plain. The mountain rose around them, dark rock and pale snow.

Anja rose too. She got to her feet, tossing her hood back and pushing her goggles up. She stood, bare-headed and bare-handed before the echo of her mountain bride. She spoke, as she had to the ghosts, in gentle tones. But her words were layered with a tenderness that made Cal blink and look away.

"Tell me what went wrong," said Anja, speaking to her goddess. "Tell me how you died."

The answer came to them not in words or visions, but in knowledge that filled every crevice of their consciousness. Cal knew the mountain's answer because for that beating moment, she *was* the mountain.

She died under boots. She died with footsteps on her back tearing the snowcaps from her flanks. She died under ice axes and pitons, strangled in rope, transfixed by steel. She died in the inexorable fall of pebbles from her ridgelines, and in avalanches that streamed down her face from those who fell too hard or shouted too loudly.

She died buried in refuse. She died beneath the tonnage of oxygen tanks and plastic wrappers and frozen human shit; beneath piss-streaked snow and bloodstained ice. She died beneath abandoned tents and forsaken fuel canisters and a thousand lost boots.

She died under their agony. Under the weight of a thousand broken spirits and abandoned dreams, under regret and guilt and disappointment. She died beneath their suffering, her glaciers soaked with the fear and pain of a thousand final moments. She died as they died, their bodies frozen to her sides like lost children seeking a warmth she could never offer. She died under the tromp of their boots, and then again under the restlessness of their spirits.

She died of their want.

Tears rolled down Cal's cheeks, and here, beyond the wind's grasp, they did not freeze. They traced hot fingers down her face and throat, and wet her lips and collar. The sadness wrapped itself around her very bones.

Anja didn't weep. "Darlin'," she said to the mountain. "Tell me how you lived."

She lived stretching for the sky. She lived leaning into the jetstream; tossing a veil of ice from her peak to watch it dance on the current of the world. She lived to carve her name against the blue. She lived for the stars that hung just out of reach and for the storms that broke themselves on her summits.

She lived for the ice that cracked her veins and split seracs from her like sloughing skin. She lived for snows that kept her secrets, buried her scars. She lived for the high loneliness, for the silence, for the company of eagles and the solitude of chasms. She lived desiring the cap of the world, the crown of the sky; she lived, seeking, wanting.

So had her ghosts.

The mountain kept what you gave her. Corpses and prayers and empty cans and *love*. The kind of love that crushed and froze and tethered. The kind of love that Cal knew all about.

Wet faced, her toes just warm enough to hurt in her boots, Cal stepped forward and stretched wide her arms.

"Great one," she said. "Let them go. Cut the line."

Behind her, through the door they had opened in the highness of the death zone, came the ghosts. They clustered at Cal's back, pressing close with their tattered Gore-Tex and black cheeks. They had flung themselves towards the sky that they might fall somewhere mighty. They took and took, and gave and gave, until all that was left were their shattered spirits and the echo of the mountain on a black plain.

Anja looked back and took Cal's hand, pulling her free of the press. She held it tight as she looked back up at the shadow mountain, and Cal braced herself against Anja's side. "Well, Mama? Will you let them go?"

For one last moment, Cal knew what it was to be the mountain and felt her answer.

Yes.

The ghosts streamed around Cal and Anja like rapids around strainers. They coursed and converged and made their way towards the peak of a mountain whose air was as thin as they were and whose spires were no sharper than their own fingers.

As the ranks of ghosts clanked on cramponed feet towards their release, Cal could have sworn that one stopped on its path and turned for a moment to look back at her. Red boots, red gloves, and a lean body all in black.

Cal raised a hand; pressed fingers to her lips.

The ghost caught her kiss in one red-glove, then turned and carried it with her to the summit.

The radio blared. "Kharo, this is base camp, do you copy?"

Kharo's answer came with a crackle of static and Cal flicked to the next channel. She'd been checking every couple of hours, but so far the only voices on the airwaves belonged to the living.

It wouldn't last. It couldn't. The mountain couldn't not be what it was, and the climbers couldn't either.

"You're brooding," Iumo rumbled, and she sighed and turned the radio off. He was sitting beside her in a canvas chair that groaned beneath his weight, feet stretched out towards the firepit as he ate a bowl of instant noodles.

"*You're* very cheerful for a man with eight fingers," Cal said, hanging the kettle on its hook over the flames; the noodles smelled amazing.

"When you offer the Bride your hand, you can't go complaining if she doesn't give it all back."

Fingers were the least of what she wouldn't give back. Hani had been airlifted to a proper hospital; his husband was with him, and Hachi's girlfriend, and Cal had left them keeping sleepless vigil around the bed.

While her friends healed, Cal had walked the cloisters with the Master Channeller, past the new mosaic, and told her that her students had been brave, a credit to her school.

She'd called Rio's mother.

She'd warmed her toes until the pain closed around her like a whiteout.

Now, she dumped an extra packet of seasoning into the bowl and ate her noodles.

Above them was the peak, unshadowed, crowned in sunlight. Awe, horror, grief and love all seemed much too big and still too small for all the mountain was to her now.

But it was a beautiful view, and Cal leaned back in her chair to appreciate it.

She found it blocked by blue robes draped over broad shoulders.

"Word is you're trekking out tomorrow," said Anja, looking down at her.

Iumo could move with a cat's grace when he chose, and he slipped from his chair so quietly Cal almost didn't catch him leaving.

"My flight's booked," Cal said. "I've been looking for you to say goodbye." The other skybrides at the monastery had shaken their heads when she'd asked for Anja, given her the same somber stares they had the first time she'd passed.

"I've had penance." Anja sounded embarrassed.

"Penance?" Cal sat upright in her chair. "But you saved everyone! You saved your Lady!"

"The Reverend Mother's set in her ways. Takes 'Don't climb the holy mountain' as less a guideline, more a commandment." Anja shook off the embarrassment as she stamped snow off her boots. "*You've* more sense than her, for all you're a heathen rabbit of a woman."

"I'll miss you too," Cal told her and meant it. Bonds formed fast and tight when you had to hang your life from them. Anja reminded her of Rio, a little. A Rio whose common sense tempered her reckless courage. The kind of woman she'd always thought Rio could become if Cal dug her nails in and hung on long enough.

"Will you be back?" Anja asked, and Cal couldn't quite tell what she wanted the answer to be.

Neverfall lived, seeking, wanting. But Cal knew what she wanted now.

"Not for the climb," she said, and Anja smiled like sunlight on snow.

Denali Stannard is the transatlantic literary partnership of Denali Hussin and Megan Stannard, represented by Saritza Hernandez of the Andrea Brown Literary Agency. Their debut work, an urban fantasy trilogy, is currently out on submission.

Denali Hussin, the top half of Denali Stannard, has worked the past decade in sustainability, climate change, and science communication. She writes The Stoop Gallants, a twice-weekly fantasy webcomic. She lives on the Rocky Mountain side of the ocean.

Megan Stannard is the back end of the literary pantomime horse that is Denali Stannard. She is a conservationist who dabbles in sword fighting, horse riding, and anything else that will make her a better writer (or fantasy protagonist. You know, if it ever comes up). She lives on the Hampstead Heath side of the ocean.

Follow their work at denalistannard.com or on social media @denalistannard.

Five Things You Should Know Before Summoning a Demon
Karl Dandenell

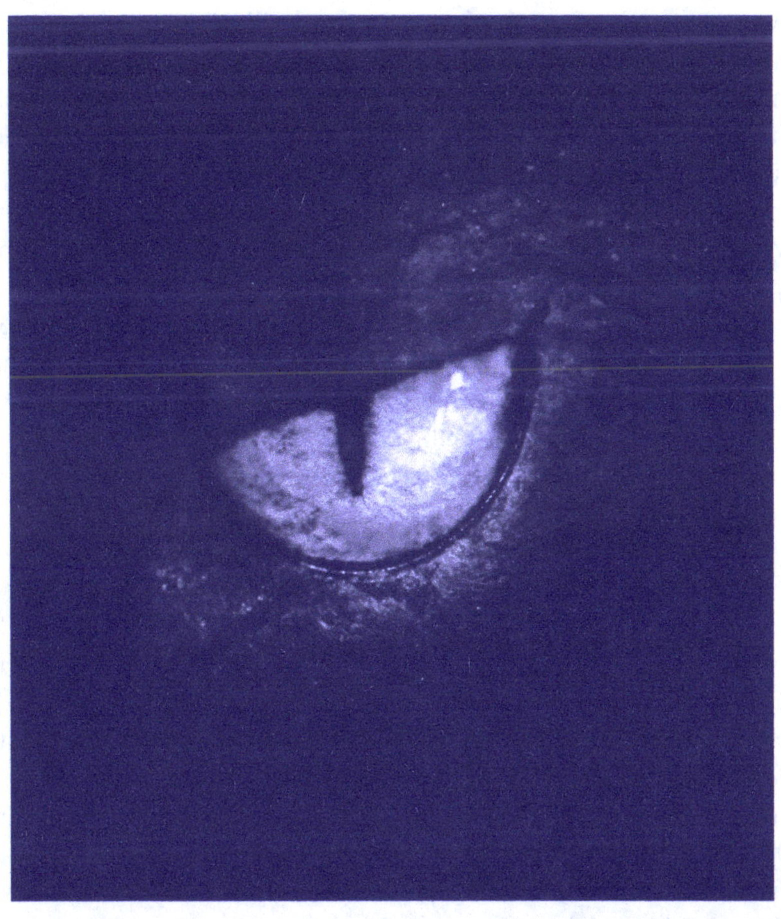

Five Things You Should Know Before Summoning a Demon

Look, if you're going to go to the trouble of summoning a demon, there are five things you need to know:

1) We Have Long, Complicated Names

This one's pretty obvious. You killed another wizard in a duel or pored over thousands of pages of ancient, nearly illegible tomes to find my name. It's pretty challenging pronouncing it with your soft mouthparts, ain't it? We aren't just "Rowena the Wise" or "Mahesh of the Ivory Fleet," although we might employ similar monikers among ourselves. Formal demon names convey our lineage, our triumphs, and our history. Truth be told, our names contain our very essence, which is the *only* reason you could hook me with your summoning spell and drag me here to this pathetic excuse for a castle.

You're lucky my name has only sixteen syllables and two glottal stops. If you want a *real* challenge, ask me how I like my venomous spines polished or what my favorite color is.

It's brown, by the way. Yellowish-brown, like fresh bile.

So do your homework and practice the demon's name before you cast your summoning, 'kay?

2) We Have Lives Too, You Know

Every wizard is surprised when I tell them this. What? Do you think we're stored in glass bottles or iron-bound chests or sealed crypts just waiting for you to drag us to the upper realms? Hardly. We have lives, rich and full. And important jobs. I myself am responsible for ten thousand slaves who *should* be digging a canal through a fetid swamp. Do you know what happens when I'm not there to crack the whip and rip off a few arms? The work just stops. Stops, I tell you. My boss—a Named Prince of the Infernal Realms—doesn't want to hear excuses.

He'll just peel off my skin and count it as my lunch break. It's all about the bottom line for him.

3) We Don't Die, But We Do Feel Pain

Look, I know you're very excited about commanding me to fight some fire-breathing lizard just so you can have its gold, or watching me slay the armored minions of your liege lord's annoying neighbor, but you have to understand something. Despite our apparent invulnerability, we still hurt. Every claw, every enchanted blade, every pool of lava hurts. Sure, we can rebuild our material forms but the process takes time and energy and boy, it smarts. I have better things to do with my day.

4) We're Supernatural, Not Stupid

When the ancient gods created the upper and lower realms, they filled them with beings both magical and mundane. Just because demons were consigned to the lower pits doesn't mean we forgot to pack our brains. We know what you're doing. You can't just order us around and expect us to roll over without a fight. And we're *definitely* not going to fall for the old "accomplish this one simple task and I'll set you free" trick. Forget about us draining the ocean or building a tower taller than the moon, or finding your lost true love. Forget it. They moved on. And so should you.

5) Seriously, Check Your Work

Demons don't belong in this realm, which is why it's no small task to summon us. First, as I already mentioned, you have to discover our name. Then you have to prepare your summoning circle with runes drawn in blood or ruby dust or what-have-you. And then you have to light the candles, in the right order, I might add. Finally, you have to command the demon to appear within the circle where you can control them.

I can't stress this last part enough. Magic isn't a natural process for you like it is for us. You can't make any mistakes.

And even if you do *everything* right, you're still dealing with a powerful, capricious, practically immortal being who would happily decorate your inner sanctum with your organs if given the opportunity.

Why? As a warning to other wizards, of course. And because it's fun.

Okay, have you got all that? Excellent.

Now, before you tell me my *really* important task, I should point out something. I've been examining your rune work and I must admit it's excellent. Really top notch. All except that third one on the left. No, your left. Looks like you forgot to close a loop. Just a little thing, really. Still, it does break the whole design, which means I've not obligated to stay inside the summoning circle.

Oopsie.

Taming Dash Nine
Mark Rigney

Taming Dash Nine

First off, can we get one thing straight? I'm a freedom fighter, not a terrorist. Second, we knew perfectly well that we'd attract the attention of a Centaur-7, and thereby hangs a tale.

Liam and I hadn't been in the Whitmore house for even twenty minutes before the Centaur clanked up the driveway and rapped its powerful alloy knuckles on the towering front door. We answered promptly, because that was expected, and if Liam's phone hadn't already been jamming the Centaur's visuals (with his very own custom-designed app, no less), that bot would have seen two medium-height, deliberately unremarkable, theoretically-but-not-actually Caucasian persons in light gray delivery coveralls, harmless service techs out to refurbish a cranky dishwasher in a lily-white neighborhood. What it saw instead is anyone's guess, since that app was hurling interference like a sandstorm flinging dust.

Now, I'm not gonna lie. The Centaur-7 is an exceptional neighborhood security device, proof positive that action really is eloquence. They've got four strong legs for speed and fence-clearing leaps, plus a muscular humanoid torso; the two long arms terminate in a pair of hands with dexterous fingers and opposable thumbs. Hidden under its various body panels, it carries an extraordinary arsenal of lethal weaponry. Only the head, squat and multi-planar, disappoints. It looks like an old outboard motor. I'm not even sure what it's for, except to house the speaker for its surprisingly resonant baritone voice. Liam claims this was an intentional ruse on the part of its New Confederation designers, an open invitation to waste your time shooting at the head when all its major sensory systems lurk elsewhere.

My point is that standing so close to a Centaur-7 is usually a recipe for certain and sudden death, but we'd tried Liam's interference trick before, first in Louisville and again in Tulsa, so we had good reason to believe we'd survive the encounter. Our role now was to be seen as legitimate appliance repair techs, the kind that would clearly blanche in the face of an inquisitive Centaur-7. It was also crucial that our facial features not be uploaded, scanned, and matched. Hence, our green-tinted contact lenses, my frizzy wig, and Liam's crumb catcher of a false mustache. Between these old-school parlor tricks and Liam's jamming app, we felt fairly confident that we had both household security and the Centaur foxed.

"Please confirm your purpose and presence," the Centaur said.

"We got a call to service a dishwasher," I replied, which was perfectly true. It was also perfectly true that we'd been waiting months for one of the Whitmore home's systems to go on the fritz so we could intercept the work order, then install listening devices. The fact that it was the dishwasher that had gone belly up was beyond our wildest hopes. Who thinks to look for listening devices in a dishwasher? Starting today, and except for those brief moments when the machine was actually running, we'd be pulling in every conversation within a forty-foot radius.

The Centaur whirred and fidgeted. Its head cocked to one side, dog-like. It was still working through various subroutines to try and clear its vision. At last it said, "Confirm your identification, please."

Like a dutiful school child, I held out the barcoder disc we'd been given at the compound's main gate. Simple things, lumpy and palm-sized, barcoder discs are designed for scanning visitors in and then out of any semi-secure setting. We use them on our side of the border, too.

At the same moment, Liam switched off his app and we both looked at our shoes. This gave the Centaur-7 a clear chance to read the barcoder with no interference. Yes, we were indeed the same two service techs who had been cleared at the gate, and we matched nicely to the cargo van we'd parked at the curb.

"Are there additional persons in the house?" the Centaur asked, as it returned the barcoder.

"Just us," I said, as Liam switched his app back on.

"Have you finished your repair?"

We had not. Liam and I are excellent covert field operatives, but dishwashers? Not our specialty. The crash course we'd undertaken over the past thirty-six hours had allowed us to extract Supply Chief Tiber Whitmore's busted heating element with relative ease, but we were some distance from installing its replacement. Besides, we'd spent the first ten minutes getting our microphone mounted. Priorities.

I explained to the Centaur that we were still diagnosing the problem, and the robot's head nodded as if considering the idea (a slick piece of programming, that; very human). At last, it said, "You expect to resolve the situation shortly."

"Just waiting on the right inspiration."

Now, I'm a big girl, so I can admit right here and right now that that was a stupid thing to say. Diagnostics and experience, that's what service techs are supposed to rely on, especially when addressing a very literal, security-minded robot. Worse, this wasn't one of the responses we'd rehearsed, and sure enough, it sent the ultra-logical Centaur-7 way off-script.

"Why," it asked, "is inspiration required in appliance repair?"

One folly breeds another. Before I could master my tongue, I heard myself say, "O, for a muse of fire, to light the brightest Heaven of invention."

Liam glared at me, and no wonder. I've been warned more than once about my tendency to improvise. Don't get me wrong, our entire battalion is proud as a peacock that I can spout other people's chestnuts like there's no tomorrow, but, as Lieutenant Kelsey made abundantly clear back when I first trained for infiltration, free association in the field can get you killed.

Well. No sooner had I let fly with my muse of fire than the Centaur made a clanking, settling noise, and did what no robot ever does: it relaxed. Its head drooped, its shoulders slumped. It didn't quite fall over, but other than that, it looked for all the world like a rag doll lapsing into a coma.

"Liam!" I whispered, completely forgetting to avoid his name. "Look!"

Liam, still nursing his conviction that he should be the one in charge, said, "What the hell did you just do?"

The robot's head tilted up and its equine hindquarters gave a sort of shimmy, as if, in the act of being startled into wakefulness, it was experiencing a muscle spasm. "Hello," it said, in a nuanced, warm, entirely novel voice. "I am Centaur Seven Dash Nine Sixty-Five. How may I be of service?"

There we stood, two badly disguised saboteurs facing down one of the deadliest security bots yet devised, and the damn thing was asking how it could help, as if it were working the front desk of a classy hotel. Assuming this had to be some kind of New Confederation trick, I wanted nothing more than to get my hands on my sidearm, but I'd left it quite intentionally in the toolbox, and the toolbox was in the kitchen. If only I'd had it in hand, I was pretty sure I could squeeze off at least two shots before the Centaur-7 either fired its Taser bolts or flat out gunned me down.

"Say something," Liam whispered.

Not gonna lie, it's hard to be both cowardly and insubordinate all in the same breath, but right there, my partner managed it.

"Centaur-7," I said, unable to remember the rest of its bewildering name, "tell me, what is your function?"

"I am programmed to carry out your commands to the best of my capability."

Liam and I traded a dark *This cannot be happening* look.

"*My* commands," I asked, "in particular?"

"You have spoken a verified Shakespearean quote, so my allegiances have now been redirected to you."

"That's one hell of an override protocol," said Liam.

"Agreed," said the Centaur-7. "It can be inferred that my founding programmer possessed both a sly wit and a wicked sense of ironic humor."

Liam swung around to me. "So, that 'muse' nonsense? That was Shakespeare?"

"Yeah. *Henry V.*"

"Precisely," said the Centaur-7. "All pre-deployment settings are now re-installed."

I said, "Okay, so what if I say something else from Shakespeare? Does that have the reverse effect?"

"Negative, but I am open to additional programming, protocols, and assignments as needed."

This really was the height of insanity. Every active United Alliance battalion spends a good chunk of its mental energy on thinking up ways to evade, trick, or disable Centaur-7 mobile security units, and here we had one ready to do our bidding, lick our hands, and (presumably) use its considerable firepower at our behest—provided, of course, that it was telling the truth.

"All right," I said, facing the robot. "This doorway is way too public. You need to get inside, and, well, I don't know. Do something that seems legit. How about you search the interior of this house? Make certain it's safe."

"Safe from what?" the Centaur-7 asked.

"Terrorists," I replied.

"I will search the premises. I will report back."

The Centaur-7 barely gave us time to clear out of its way as it trotted through the doorway and began its sweep of the house. I'd never seen a Centaur-7 indoors before, and it looked a good deal larger when hemmed in by four clean white walls. Frankly, it also looked ridiculous, nosing around Supply Chief Whitmore's ostentatious, to-the-manor-born stairway as if it were a dog sniffing out trouble.

"Robin," Liam said, as he pulled the door closed behind us, "this could be a major-league opportunity."

That was surely true, but I didn't appreciate his phrasing. Baseball's Major League hadn't operated in at least a decade. During the war, nearly every stadium on both sides had been converted to field hospitals. Not a pretty end to America's pastime, or my one-time games of catch with my dad.

As the Centaur clopped off to explore the living room, Liam caught my wrist. "I'm not kidding. If we can get this thing home…"

"Home? You want to bring a Centaur-7 back to the nest, maybe over the border?"

"If we can disassemble it, figure out what makes it tick—Robin, this is our chance to learn the damn thing's weaknesses."

I gave him my I'm-in-charge stare. "We just learned its weakness. Shakespeare."

"That can't be system-wide." Then he checked his own logic. "Although, I guess if it isn't system-wide, then the odds of our meeting the exact one we can trigger? Beyond astronomical."

"Trillions to one, sure—unless the whole fleet was set up by one guy, some crank in a lab who didn't like where society was heading and sneaked in a few lines of code to basically say 'Up yours' to the New Confederation."

Looking grim, Liam nodded. "Which is why we have to assume we're being pranked. There is every chance that thing will saunter back into the kitchen, guns blazing, and that'll be that."

I thought this over. The notion that the Centaur had been programmed to trick us was far more plausible than the notion that we'd sprung the lock on a highly whimsical fail-safe, some wacky Easter egg left behind by its original code-master.

"Well," I said, "if its main goal is to kill us, it's had ample opportunity, and if it's trying to lure us into giving up compromising intel, then why is it hiding out in a whole different room?"

Liam shrugged. "No clue."

"Let's get this dishwasher closed back up, so we can get out of here."

"Do you think it'll fit in the van?"

"What, the dishwasher?"

"No! The Centaur."

I lifted my cap, adjusted my idiotic wig, and jammed the cap back on. I had no doubt that the Centaur-7 could fold itself into the back of our service van, but maybe not without ditching half of our tools, not to mention hardware and replacement parts, many of which had taken long months to scrounge.

"Liam," I said, "you deal with the heating element. I'm gonna have a chat with our new friend."

I left Liam in the clutches of the dishwasher and headed off to find the Centaur. Not a difficult task. Centaurs weren't built for stealth, and I could easily hear it tromping around the voluminous living room. When I arrived, it was checking under the throw pillows, searching, presumably, for terrorists. Very small terrorists.

After watching for a moment, I said, "I need to know if you're in cell or sat communication with other Centaur units."

"No," it said, in a dejected tone. "Those links were severed when my protocols were re-set."

"So, you're not in communication with security staff for this compound."

"Negative."

I pressed the point. "Are you sending a passive data stream? Of any sort?"

The Centaur cocked its head in my direction. "I am in active communication with myself, and with you. At the present time, that is all."

"How do I know you aren't lying?"

"My current protocols do not permit the dissemination of falsehoods."

My eyes rolled like the snarky teen I used to be (and not that long ago, either). "How can I trust what you just said?"

The robot considered this for far longer than its processors required. "Without connecting you to one or more of my data ports, I do not see that assertions of truth may be proven. Disinformation is the central problem of the machine condition."

I grinned despite myself. The damned thing sounded downright glum.

Brightening, the Centaur said, "Shall I continue to search for terrorists? Or should we enter into a philosophical debate? I am familiar with the relevant passages in Hume, Aristotle, the Koran, and many others."

"I need to think," I said. "So yes, search, and I'll tag along."

From the kitchen, I heard banging, hammering, and a loud curse, and I resisted an urge to rejoin Liam. Instead, the Centaur and I worked our way into a series of tidy offices, cozy guest bedrooms, and jealousy-inducing bathrooms. It's not like we live so badly back in the nest, but this was luxury of a significantly higher order.

"Okay," I said, "so you're not in communication with any outside systems. What about the house?"

"Supply Chief Whitmore's household AI systems are rudimentary in the extreme."

I frowned. This was a very upscale neighborhood, reserved for military command and ranking civil servants. Tiber Whitmore's home could, through voice command or remote text, do everything that had been promised back in the interactive dawn of the 21st century, and quite a bit more besides. Rudimentary? Well, perhaps it was, to a Centaur-7.

"Hey," I said, "remind me of your name."

"My official designation is too long for most humans to remember. You may call me Dash Nine. What do I call you?"

"Robin."

"Just Robin?"

"If you want titles, I'm Field Ops Corporal Robin Dell."

The robot nodded once, apparently satisfied.

"All right," I said. "Dash Nine, get in touch with the house and locate the safe, if there is one."

"The safe," said Dash Nine, without hesitation, "is in the basement, in the billiards room, behind the liquor cabinet."

"While we're at it, scramble the household video and audio logs for the previous hour, and order it to continue that protocol until we leave."

"Done."

"Great. Now, let's shift our terrorist search to the basement."

It turns out that watching a Centaur-7 clump down a staircase has real entertainment value. Definitely not a picture of grace. However, Dash Nine totally made up for that by instantly extracting the safe's combination from the home security system, and once we were in, I took everything, every last folder, I.D., and data drive. So what if Lieutenant Kelsey had ordered us not to deviate from the basic assignment of installing a single listening device? That train had long since left the station.

As I closed up the safe, being careful not to leave prints, Dash Nine tilted its head toward the ceiling and said, very calmly, "A terrorist has arrived."

I was trying to wrangle my loose armload of intel (the billiards room was kind of shy on bags and boxes). "Where?" I said. "How do you know?"

"'Knowledge makes a king most like his maker.'"

"You want to try that again?"

"The terrorist is in the driveway, now exiting a red pickup truck. I am cognizant of this because I did not interfere with the external feed from the household security cameras."

"And you're still tapped into the system."

"Correct."

I got a better grip on the loose grab-bag of files and said, "Was that more Shakespeare? That knowledge-king quote?"

"Of course. Now, if you'll follow me, I will take us by the most direct route to intercept the terrorist."

Dash Nine didn't wait for a response, and by the time my new best bud reached the front door, I was lagging far behind. Plus, I had to make a quick detour to the kitchen.

"Forget the dishwasher and get these stowed," I said to Liam, who was sitting cross-legged on the floor, parts and tools strewn around him like a tiny bomb blast. Without waiting for an answer, I dumped my armload on the nearest counter and ran for the door.

As I arrived, Dash Nine spun its head one hundred and eighty degrees and said, "The terrorist has stopped approximately three point four six meters from the door. Shall I open up, or open fire?"

"Wait, how do you even know this person's a terrorist?"

"The subject is Latinx, male, and is wearing a New Confederation limitation collar."

Now that was a mouthful. Given the collar, the man on the far side of the door was almost certainly one of those unfortunates who'd gotten caught on the wrong side of the Mexican border when the war broke out, and he hadn't had a green card, or at least not an updated visa, and now he was an indentured servant: fed, housed, and cared for by the benevolent New Confederation. Just to make sure he stayed put and stayed servile, his new masters had kindly outfitted him with one seriously punitive gizmo.

"Dash Nine," I said, "this guy sounds harmless."

"Agreed," said Dash Nine, sounding newly sheepish and even a touch disappointed, "but you instructed me to look for terrorists, and this is the closest we've come so far."

From the kitchen, I heard Liam's plaintive voice asking what was going on. To Dash Nine, I said, "Do not open fire unless I directly order it. Clear?"

"I will not cry havoc, or let loose the dogs of war, unless you insist."

Good enough for me. I hauled open the door.

On the far side stood a heavy-set, weather-beaten man wearing a plaid work shirt, a wide straw hat to keep off the sun, and a pristine limitation collar, pale-blue. In one hand, he held a pair of rust-pocked garden clippers, and when I appeared, he looked up, surprised.

Apparently, the primary targets of his nefarious terror plot were the rose bushes on either side of the front walk.

"Oh," I said. "Hi."

The man looked from Dash Nine to me and back again. He slowly raised his hands, presumably thinking he was under arrest. "Whatever I did," he said, his accent light and musical, "I didn't do it."

Ignoring this, I looked along the street, both ways. Liam wasn't actively jamming anything now, and I was kicking myself for so blithely putting myself in view of who knew how many additional cameras and scanner feeds. At least there wasn't any traffic, and no sign of additional Centaur-7s.

Dash Nine leaned close to my ear and spoke in the robot equivalent of a clandestine whisper. "If he is a terrorist, I stand ready to unleash a killing frost."

The man on the doorstep clearly registered this as a lethal threat, and the garden clippers nearly fell from his fingers. "Please, no," he said, and he squeezed his eyes tightly shut.

How had my day veered so far off course? This whole caper had been designed from the ground up to be the most straightforward of missions. Instead? One change-up after another. The safest course would have been to sacrifice this guy for the cause—wrong place, wrong time, an unfortunate casualty of war. But, as Lieutenant Kelsey is fond of pointing out, I've got a stupidly soft heart, and here I stood, facing an enslaved human being, one that I might have the power to help.

Keeping my hat brim low, I said, "*¿Como se llama?*"

"*Me llamo Mateo Orozco. No lo hice, en serio.*"

It occurred to me that he probably couldn't say anything much more controversial than that without setting off the collar. "Okay," I said, "put your hands down. You're here for what, yard work? *¿Las flores?*"

He gestured at the scraggly, unloved roses as if they were the greatest disappointment of his life. "*Las rosas, si. Estan enfermas.* You call it 'black spot.'"

My mother had kept roses before the war, and she'd taught me the basics. No doubt about it, the Whitmore's roses needed help in a big way, but I wasn't sure I cared; the Supply Chief's flower beds didn't qualify as politically neutral.

To Dash Nine, I said, "Is this guy recording us?"

"Confirmed," Dash Nine responded, with a quick nod of its featureless head. "The limitation collar records constantly. It is unlikely, however, that anyone is listening."

"So, it's a passive feed?"

"Approximately five percent of the time, at random, the subject will be observed directly by either human or robot moderators."

I thought about those odds. They seemed pretty great, but not great enough.

Dash Nine inched closer. "Shall I deactivate his communication channels?"

"You can do that?"

"All Centaur-7 units have authorization to access limitation collars."

"Even though we brought you back to your factory settings."

Dash Nine nodded again. "I was disconnected from standard network channels, but all passwords remain functional."

This presented a conundrum. If Dash Nine blocked or switched off the man's collar, that would set off alarms all over the compound. Talk about attracting attention. But if I didn't give that order? If we got out of the compound without trouble, there'd be no reason for anyone to go back and scan through whatever Mateo's collar had already recorded. On the other hand, if pretty much anything went south, I'd already left a virtual ton of compromising data, including the fact that I had somehow tamed a Centaur. Assuming, of course, that I really had.

"Hey, partner!" I called, aiming my voice toward the kitchen, and deliberately avoiding Liam's name. "We need to make tracks!"

He responded with, "On my way!"

I turned back to Mateo. "You got family here?"

Shaking his head, Mateo said, "Here? No. Juarez, and some in El Paso."

La Ciudad Juarez: still under Mexican control. El Paso: still a free city. Either one would be better than here.

To Mateo, I said, "If we get you past New Confederation lines, do you think you could reach El Paso? Would you want to try?"

Mateo's eyes narrowed. I could all but see his racing thoughts. *Should I trust this woman? Or will trusting get me killed?*

Behind me, Dash Nine cleared its non-existent throat. "If we are continuing this conversation, it really might be best to shut down the link-ups to Señor Orozco's collar."

"Once we do that," I said, "we are on the move and making a run for it."

In chatty tones, Dash Nine said, "In case it helps you reach a decision, I must inform you that a fellow Centaur-7 unit is one block away and headed in our direction."

"To this exact address?"

"Network chatter suggests that my signal-silence has attracted attention. This visit represents the first stage of what will become an ever-increasing response. Shall I create a diversion?"

"Um, sure. But how about something not in view of here?"

Sounding downright smug, Dash Nine said, "I must report that the swimming pool pump at 344 Honeysuckle has just experienced an unfortunate and quite spectacular malfunction."

This was the kind of robot I could get sweet on in a hurry. "Liam!" I called. "What's the hold-up?"

"I don't have enough hands!"

Bot-crush or no, it struck me that if Dash Nine were yanking my chain, this was the moment it would turn on us, and as I jogged to the kitchen to help Liam wrangle our gear, I half-expected to feel a sudden spray of bullets. But no. Nothing happened. Liam had our tools ready, and he'd found a sack to stow what I'd dragged from the safe. The dishwasher, with its immaculate stainless steel door closed up, looked peaceful, harmless, but since I hadn't given Liam time to finish, it was probably full of loose parts. No matter. What we had from the safe was intel on a much grander scale—or so I hoped.

At the door, we did a check for overhead drones, found none, and made an orderly retreat to the van. Vans are funny things. There's more room inside than you'd ever believe, and somehow, by bending its torso forward like some long-necked lizard, Dash Nine fit without our having to ditch any inventory. At the very back, Mateo squeezed between Dash Nine's hooves, and in another moment, with me at the wheel, we were on our way.

After two minutes of leisurely driving, we were in sight of the compound's main gate, the same one we'd entered by not an hour before. Liam had his phone out, ready to jam the gatekeeper's feed, but Dash Nine stretched its head forward and said, "'When great leaves fall, the winter is at hand.'"

"Dash," I said, "that's not really helpful."

"What I mean to say," said the robot, "is that the gatekeeper's kiosk is currently occupied by a human."

Liam sat forward, straining to see. "No, it's a bot. It's *always* a bot!"

"The Semblance-4 typically on duty has experienced a temporary electrical malfunction."

I kept driving, and glanced at Liam. "Coincidence?"

"'Coincidences,'" intoned Dash Nine, "'are spiritual puns.'"

Liam and I responded one over top of the other. I said, "What does that even mean?" and Liam, annoyed, said, "That's not Shakespeare."

Sounding affronted, Dash Nine said, "'A foolish consistency is the hobgoblin of little minds.'"

One hand on the wheel, I waved the other in frustration. "That's not Shakespeare, either!"

"In point of fact," said Dash Nine, "I was referencing G.K. Chesterton. Poet, etc. 'Master of paradox.'"

I gave Dash Nine's shoulder a hard shove. "How about you just duck down and keep out of sight?"

"Of course. Operation Duck and Cover, commencing now." Dash Nine retracted itself, and Mateo let out a distant squawk, a reminder that we were tightly packed.

"Everyone stay calm," I said, as I nudged the van over the traffic spikes—no backing out now—and up to the kiosk. Two yards from my front bumper was a simple wooden gate-arm, striped like a candy cane, with a stop sign attached. That wasn't our problem. Three yards beyond that stood a much more substantial gate, eight feet high, black as night, anchored into the compound's wall on both sides, and made of reinforced steel. It reminded me of a coffin lid, seen from the inside.

The kiosk window slid open and a disheveled young woman leaned out, caught in the act of pinning on a name badge. Instead of a standard issue New Confederation jacket, she wore a white button-down like an old-fashioned airline pilot. The patch on her shoulder said "JobTrackers."

I couldn't believe it. To cover for the faulty Semblance-4, the compound had hired a temp.

"Wow!" said the woman. "Beautiful day, huh? I think I'm supposed to see your barcoder?"

I handed it over, and the disc beeped obligingly as she ran the code. All smiles, she said, "Gosh, look at that. It works." Then one of her half-dozen data screens gave her pause. Brow furrowing, she said, "You were at 3644, the Whitmore residence?"

"Yes, ma'am."

"I'm getting a report about a Centaur-7 dispatched to that address that hasn't been responding."

"I'm sure I don't know anything about that."

Next to me, Liam leaned forward, positioning himself to pull a revolver from under the seat. This idiot temp had no idea how close she was to taking a bullet to the head. Another thing she probably didn't know: we were on the clock. Once a barcoder gets scanned, there's a two-minute window to open the compound gate, after which the gate puts itself on lockdown and won't open under any circumstances for a full half hour.

"Bizarre," the woman said, and she rolled a fingertip across the ridgeline of her lower teeth. "Centaur-7s, they don't just...vanish. Do they?"

Lieutenant Kelsey's primary admonition was playing on repeat in my head, *We are not terrorists. We are freedom fighters.*

"Robin," Liam whispered. He was all but begging to end this encounter with a bullet, but before I could decide, Mateo's collar finally figured out he wasn't where he was supposed to be. It let out a chilling rattlesnake hiss and Mateo began screaming as if he were being burned alive.

"Dash!" I yelled, "Shut it down!"

In the same moment, Liam pulled his revolver and did his best to line up a clear shot at the kiosk. As Mateo's collar went silent (well done, Dash), I lunged for Liam's arm, hoping to disrupt his aim.

"Dash!" I cried again, and damned if that robot didn't read my mind. Before Liam could fend me off, Dash dove forward and clamped a single metal hand to Liam's shoulder. I saw (and felt) a flash of blue electricity, and Liam went limp, gulping twice before falling sideways against the glove compartment.

"Don't worry," Dash said, over Mateo's ongoing, rhythmic whimpers. "I will monitor your partner's cardiac activity. I will also monitor Mateo, the gardener who is not a terrorist. You deal with the gate."

"You can't open it?"

"Negative. The compound gate is disconnected from all network feeds. You have to press the button."

I turned my attention to the kiosk, where the cowering temp was staring right at me, too terrified to look away. Because the kiosk was set (by design, I'm sure) too close to the pavement, I couldn't open the driver's side door, which left me with one option and one only: the truth.

"Listen," I said, "here's the deal. We're the terrorists you've heard so much about. United Alliance, in the flesh. The enemy. But we've got family and friends, just like you, and right now, you've got about thirty seconds to open that gate before it triggers an alarm, and if that alarm goes off, everyone in this van dies, and so will you, because New Confederation intelligence services will have every reason to question you, and even if they don't kill you in the process, you'll wish they had. But, if my friends and I roll out of here peacefully, no one will have any reason to question you about anything. So, I am begging you. It's a win-win if you press that button."

In a sandpaper whisper, the woman said, "I should call security."

"Fifteen seconds," I said.

I couldn't see her hands, but her left arm reached toward her control panel.

"Come on," I said, exhorting her. "Screw your courage to the sticking-place."

She blinked, surprised. "I remember that. We read it in school. *MacBeth.*"

"Ten seconds," I said. It was only an estimate, but I needed a prod––and it worked. Her arm shifted, angling toward a different button.

She pressed it. The gate groaned with the effort and notched upward; a strip of daylight rose along its base, as bright white as a sunlit snowscape.

Do people truly breathe sighs of relief? I know I did.

The temp rubbed a hand over her mouth and said, as I shifted the van into drive, "Let me come with you."

"You jump ship, they'll be on our tail in seconds."

"I could help. I could fight!"

The wooden gate swung upwards as its huge metal counterpart reached its full height and clanked to a stop. We had a free shot to the highway.

"You want to fight?" I said. "Then stay here, and don't give us away."

"But I want to come with you!"

She looked ready to shimmy through the kiosk window, and from there into the van. If she tried, I'd have to push her back, maybe even shoot her—which gave me an idea.

"Dash," I said, "can you lean forward enough to take her picture?"

An extension rod like an old antenna snaked out of Dash's shoulder, narrowly missing my head. "Done," Dash said. "Also, the gate will close in twelve seconds."

I turned back to the temp. "What's your name?"

Eyes welling, sniffling, she said, "Kayla."

"Okay, listen. Kayla. We've got your photo, which means we can track you. And on another day, with planning, we can run you to our side of the border. But it can't be now."

I hit the gas without waiting for a reply; covert wars just don't have time for the poetry of fare-thee-well. In another moment, we were past the gate and gone, mission accomplished.

Sort of.

In short order, we'd rendezvous with our pit crew, switch vehicles, and be back at the nest in time for lunch. Mateo would be sent to tactical, where they'd work on removing his collar. Liam would head to the infirmary, leaving me to face down a nasty debriefing. I figured the odds were high that I'd get tossed out of field work for good, but frankly, I was pretty sure I deserved a medal. I mean, who else ever brought home a working (and downright friendly) Centaur-7?

"Hey, Dash," I said, as the compound faded in the rear-view mirror, "how's Liam?"

"Vitals are normal, but I doubt he'll wake any time soon."

I nodded. It occurred to me that Liam might be trouble, in future. It was entirely possible I'd made myself a long-term enemy. If that were the case, it would be doubly unfortunate, since in the long years before I got promoted to Field Ops Corporal, Liam and I had been friends.

To Dash Nine, I said, "You know, when we get back, some of the lab techs are gonna want to take you apart."

Dash Nine shifted restlessly. "You will not let them."

"Buddy, the day someone cuts into you, it's over my dead body."

Machines don't laugh, but Dash Nine managed a pretty good approximation. Then it said, "Are you familiar with *Casablanca*?"

"Say what?"

My hulking killer robot laughed again. "Robin, I do believe this is the start of a beautiful friendship."

My derision came out as a snort. "Either that, or this is a seriously complicated ruse to get me to drive you back to the nest. And once there, you lay waste to everyone in sight."

For a long moment, Dash Nine said nothing.

"Dash," I said, "tell me that's not what's happening here."

One of the Centaur-7's better processors let out a wonderfully human sigh. "Is it possible," said Dash Nine, "that I understand friendship better than you?"

Mark Rigney has had over fifty short pieces find print in a gentle arc covering the last two decades, with stories in Lightspeed, Realms of Fantasy, and more. Theatrical credits, too, with play across the U.S., including off-Broadway, along with Canada, Hong Kong, Nepal, and Australia.

Seventy Miles from Phoenix

David Dixon

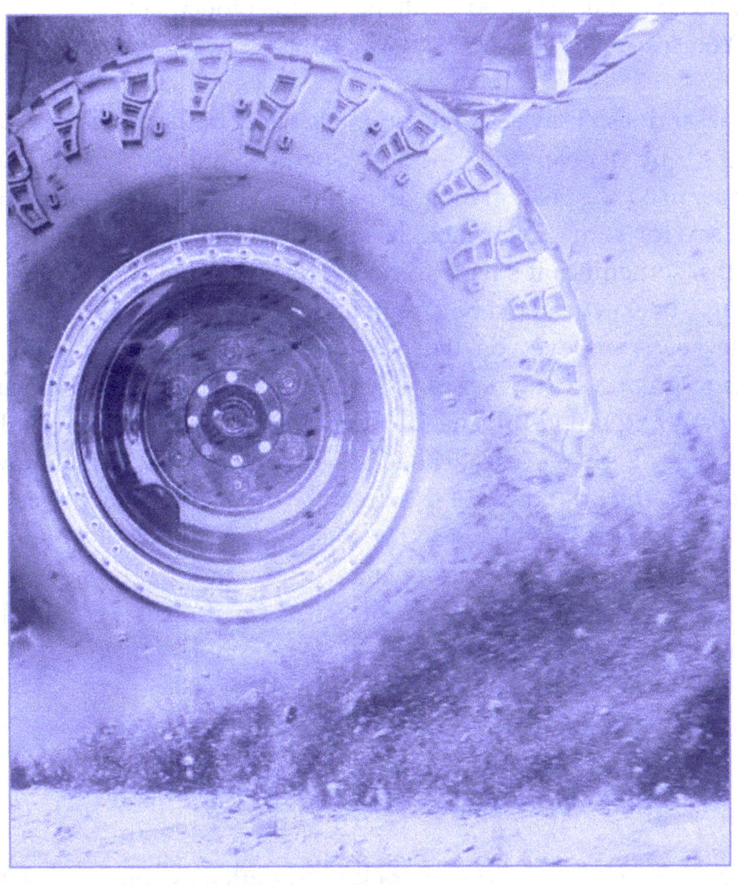

Seventy Miles from Phoenix

Michael squints as he stares west down I-10, snapped like a black chalk line across the parched brown desert. The rising heat blurs the horizon into shimmering waves, and I-10 vanishes skyward, blending into undulating black lines, an infinite series of distant, writhing snakes.

"See it?" Caesar says.

"No."

"It's coming."

Caesar would see it. After all, he has the binoculars.

"You sure?"

"*Si.*"

Caesar doesn't say anything else. That isn't unusual; the heat sucks the life out of everything—plants, people, animals, conversation. Michael used to speak in more than monosyllables, he thinks, but he can't say for sure. Even though he's only been in the RT for a few months, sometimes it's hard to remember what life was like back in Chicago, back when he'd been soft, back when living was easy.

He keeps his eyes on the horizon, squinting even though he's wearing polarized sunglasses. He glances at Caesar, his binoculars now dangling around his neck. Caesar never squints, even without sunglasses. Early on, Michael had asked him how he did that, how he stared into the brightness of the desert without flinching. "*Porque no soy una pequeña perra*" had been his answer.

Michael didn't ask Caesar too many questions after that.

After another minute of silence, Michael finally sees it: a dark speck on the horizon, rippling in the heat and growing larger.

A truck.

"I see it," he says.

"Good."

Caesar passes him the binoculars, and Michael trains them on the truck.

It's a big one, hauling four trailers one after the other, barrelling down I-10 at ninety miles an hour. The tractor itself is sleek and black and bullet-shaped, and Michael can just make out the Alibaba logo on its aerodynamic shell.

"What kind is it?" Caesar asks.

Michael adjusts the binoculars and strains to find a manufacturer's logo. "I dunno, can't tell." He finds a red oval with writing low on the shell, but he can't hold the binoculars steady enough to read it. "There's a red circle—oval, really—and there's writing, but I can't tell what—"

"Peterbilt," Caesar says. "Is there a sensor pod up high? Left or right side?"

Michael scans upwards. "Left side."

"Whip antennas or dish?" Caesar asks. "Toward the back. Might even be on the first trailer."

"Ahhh… looks like whip antennas. Two of 'em, other side of the sensor pod."

Caesar grunts.

Michael has spent enough weeks around Caesar to know that isn't good. He looks away from the binoculars. "What?"

"Can't ride it," Caesar says. He casts a worried glance up at the sun, high and merciless overhead. "We gotta go back soon. Half an hour more, maybe."

Michael takes another look at the truck with his binoculars, now close enough for him to read the registration stickers down the side. Unlike some of the rigs he's seen before, it doesn't have anti-climb spikes, or roof ridges that make it impossible to rest on top. "Why not? What's wrong with it? No anti-ride gear on it. I thought you said this morning that—"

"It's a Trump Truck, *ese*. It don't *need* gear. The other trucks? Yeah, sure. But a Trump Truck don't need it 'cuz you can't stop it. You try to get in its way and—" Caesar smashes a tattooed fist into his brown, calloused palm.

"I thought you said they had to stop. This morning, before we left camp, you said we could stop one easy," Michael protests. He's sweating—well, he's been sweating because that's all anybody does in the RT, but now he's *really* sweating. It's a three-hour walk back to camp, and they made the trek out here mostly under the cover of darkness. The thought of walking back in daylight doesn't sit well at all.

"Most of 'em, they do gotta stop. But not the Trump Trucks. When that fine-ass bitch was President, she had 'em change the rules, but only for those four years, you know? So you gotta be careful, gotta pay attention, *ese*. Anything from '32 to '36, you gonna get crushed. Last mistake anybody ever makes in the RT, trying to ride a Trump Truck."

"Shit," Michael mutters.

"Yeah."

The truck is bearing down on them now, the musical hum of its tires growing louder as it nears. It gives a cursory blast of its horn when it comes within a half a mile of them, but doesn't slow. Michael snaps his head to look as it zips past, bringing a welcome blast of wind in its wake. The breeze isn't cool, given that the temperature hovers near 140 degrees, but at least it breaks up the oppressive stillness of the desert.

Caesar stares after it a moment before he picks up his dusty olive-drab rucksack and cinches it to his back. Next comes his anti-drone rifle, used to keep prying eyes away from Caesar's extralegal activities. The rifle consists of a pair of four-foot-long, flat antennas about three inches wide connected by homemade wiring to a bulky battery in the stock, the whole thing held together by duct tape and hatred, judging by the curses in Spanish and English stenciled down the side of the antennas. Caesar slings it over his shoulder and nods south, back the way they came. "Come on. No point waiting any longer. I thought we'd already be gone. Must be a slow day for rich people ordering shit."

"I thought you said we had half an hour more," Michael says. Caesar shrugs.

Michael sighs, dreading the grueling walk back to camp. Before he reaches for his own backpack, though, he takes one more look west through the binoculars. A smile cracks his sun-chapped lips.

"There's another truck."

Caesar extends a hand, and Michael gives him the heavy, rubber-coated binoculars so he can scope out their prey.

"Get ready, *mijo*."

That's a good sign. Caesar only calls anybody *mijo* when he's in a good mood.

Michael unzips his pack and takes out the metallic space blanket Caesar gave him to carry, along with a can of yellow spray paint. He unfolds the blanket across the middle of the eastbound lanes, wincing as it reflects the sunlight like a mirror. "All right, I got—"

"Remember what I said?" Caesar asks. "Put the circles *before* the lines, 'cuz if you fuck it up and—"

"I remember," Michael interrupts. They'd only been over it a hundred times.

"Okay. Then what the hell you doin' standing here?" Caesar asks.

Michael shakes his head and mutters a curse, then grabs the paint and starts to jog west toward the approaching truck.

"Yo," Caesar calls. "Don't forget your water. It's farther than you think. I ain't dragging your ass back."

Michael pulls a plastic two-quart canteen from a side pouch in his backpack, takes a swallow of water so hot it's sweet, then slings it over his side with a strap and takes off down the interstate.

By the time he's made it an eighth of a mile, Michael is glad Caesar told him to bring the canteen. He's sweating so hard now that it's pouring down his face, stinging his eyes, and the brief jog in the heat is enough to make him gasp for breath. He takes another swig before he keeps on jogging until he reaches what he reckons to be the quarter mile Caesar has insisted on. There, he uses the spray paint to decorate the road with a pair of two-foot yellow circles four feet apart, followed by a pair of heavy yellow lines.

By now, the truck is close enough for Michael to see that it's an Amazon Prime truck in blue and white livery, but he can't make out what the make and model are. Still, if Caesar says it'll stop, he knows it will.

Michael sprints back to the space blanket as the truck draws closer. The stifling heat is ever present, and running makes it that much worse. He feels his meager breakfast rising in his throat.

"Careful now, *mijo*," Caesar calls with a smile from where he stands in the middle of the space blanket.

For a moment, Michael hesitates. Caesar watches him, his dark brown eyes revealing nothing, but Michael knows what he's thinking.

This is a test of sorts. Caesar doesn't need Michael to stop the truck. Hell, Caesar has done it by himself a hundred times, probably. But

Michael knows it's not about that. Caesar has been good to him since he's come to the RT, and here the RT, you live and die by three things—your friends, your word, and your guts. But the first two aren't worth a damn without the last one, and that's what Caesar is looking to find.

Michael steps into the eastbound lanes and stands next to Caesar, staring into the face of the oncoming truck as it speeds toward them. Michael's heart pounds, even though he knows it shouldn't, even though he knows he can trust Caesar to get it right.

When the truck reaches Michael's painted marks, the truck's brakes whine as it recoups some of the braking energy for the motor's batteries. Michael grins, and his heart rate slows a bit.

The truck's sensors pick them up, and it honks three times in protest as it comes to a complete stop fifteen feet in front of them. The truck's electric motor is silent, save for a fan whirring somewhere deep inside the tractor, cocooned completely in its aerodynamic cowl.

"See? Works every time," Caesar says, nodding at the space blanket. He'd explained it to Michael back at camp last week. Even though the trucks were programmed to stop for any pedestrians in the road, sometimes their cameras had a little difficulty picking people out against the asphalt—Caesar seemed to think the companies did it on purpose—but the metallic space blanket highlighted the contrast and made sure the autopilot recognized them as people. The paint symbols he'd sent Michael to lay down warned the truck of potential pedestrians ahead, which sent it into its more cautious, big-city safe mode instead of its normal high-speed long-haul mode.

"Never doubted you," Michael says.

Caesar barks a laugh. "You were ready to shit your pants. *No la mientas a un mentiroso.* Now, fold up the blanket but don't move just yet."

Michael does as instructed while Caesar tosses a rope ladder with heavy earth magnets on one end up to the roof of the first trailer.

"Caution," the truck warns loudly in a disembodied female voice. "Attempting to ride, hijack, damage, or otherwise interfere with the operation of this automated truck is a crime, and will subject you to criminal penalties which vary by jurisdiction. Additionally, you will be subject to civil penalties by Amazon Incorporated, and your Prime membership will be canceled if you are a member."

"I know, baby," Caesar says to the truck, patting the tractor's fiberglass shell. "But I ain't a member, so I could give a fuck." He tugs on the rope ladder, which doesn't move, then walks back to Michael. "Grab your shit, *ese*. Time to ride."

Michael stuffs the blanket back into his pack, then throws it over his shoulders. He takes Caesar's place in front of the truck while Caesar straps on his rucksack and hoists his drone-rifle. Caesar climbs the ladder to the trailer roof and looks down over the front of the tractor.

"All right, we're good. When you get about five feet behind the sensor pod—" he jerks his head towards a sleek bulbous shape high on the left side of the tractor "—she'll start to move, so don't be surprised. Climb on up. They take a little time to get going."

Michael nods and trots to the ladder. Just as Caesar predicted, the truck starts to roll almost as soon as he's no longer in front of it, but Michael has no problem climbing the thirty feet to the top of the trailer. Once he gets there, he's pleased to find a pair of makeshift reclining chairs bolted to the trailer roof, allowing him to lie down comfortably and still be tucked below the top of the tractor's cowl so there's no danger of being blown off when the truck is at full speed.

"She's a slut." Caesar pats the trailer beneath them as the truck picks up speed. "Been ridden a lot. Nice to have these seats on your first trip, but don't get used to it."

"I'm surprised they don't take 'em off." Michael slides into one, rolling halfway over so he can shrug off his backpack, which he secures to a hook someone has attached to the seat for just that purpose.

"They do," Caesar answers. "When they find 'em. But these things drive and park themselves, and the maintenance and loading and shit is all robot, too, so it's not like they're really getting a lot of eyes on it, you know?" Caesar takes a swig of his canteen, tucks his hands behind his head, and closes his eyes. He's asleep in seconds.

Michael tries to do the same, and between the air rushing around him to keep him cool and the shade of the cowl over his head, he expects to find it easy to sleep, but, unlike Caesar, he's not used to the motion or the noise, so he stays awake.

He keeps his eyes closed and thinks of Chicago and his mom's warning when he told her he was heading to the Restricted Territory.

He can't help but smile. Sure, there were some rough times early on, but he's been with Caesar and his crew for a month, and he'd make more in a year with him than he'd make in a decade working some dead-end shift job up in Chicago competing with robots for his bread—if he'd managed to get a job at all.

Something interrupts the sun's light for a moment, and Michael's blood runs cold. His eyes snap open. Birds were rare this far south these days, which can only mean one thing.

Drones.

"Caesar, man, wake up," Michael shouts over the roar of the wind, sitting up and using his hand to shield his eyes as he scans the cloudless blue sky. I think we got some eyes on us."

Caesar is awake in a flash, and already reaching for his drone-rifle. "Fuck."

"Yeah."

They scan the sky for several minutes, but the drone doesn't reappear.

"You sure you saw one?" Caesar asks.

"I mean… no, not exactly," Michael says, feeling stupid. "But there was a shadow, and I figure that—"

"Yeah, it does," Caesar says. "But it might not be watching the road. There's other types, too."

Michael nods, looking back over the next four trailers strung out behind the one they're on, and looking farther back down the arrow-straight strip of I-10 behind them. "How long to Phoenix?" he asks, leaning close so Caesar can hear him. He'll feel better when they reach the city. Officially, it's abandoned, like the rest of the RT, but at least there the surveillance drones find it harder to track people among the skeletons of the skyscrapers.

Caesar doesn't answer. Instead, he pokes his head around the left side of the truck, exposing his face to the full force of the wind before retreating back under the fiberglass shield. "Not much longer," he says, leaning close to Michael. "Highway 60 is coming up in a mile or two, off to the left. From there it's like a hundred miles to Phoenix, tops. So, like, maybe an hour or so."

Caesar lies back down and is asleep in no time again, but Michael drinks some water and eats a long-expired energy bar to quiet his growling stomach. He's lost a lot of weight since he came to the RT, but he still can't match Caesar's seemingly unflagging energy no matter the heat or lack of food and water. He stares off to the west, wondering if they'll ever have reason to go all the way to the coast. He'd like that, he thinks. He's never seen the ocean except on TV, and even though the Great Lakes are *like* the ocean, they *aren't* the ocean.

Something catches his eye behind them, and he cocks his head to the side to stare at it. There's another vehicle on the road, but it doesn't look big enough to be a truck and—

His heart almost stops.

Flashing lights.

"Caesar, Caesar," he shouts. "The cops!"

Again, Caesar startles awake, and this time there's no denying it. They've been made, somehow. "*Ay chingados*," he mutters. "Okay, *ese*, listen up. Here's how it's gonna be. When he gets close, he's gonna send his magic 5-0 signal and the truck is gonna stop. When it slows down to like twenty miles an hour, we jump. He won't look for us if we head off into the desert because he really doesn't care. He just wants us off the truck. But if he catches us while we're still aboard? That shit ain't good, *ese*."

"*Jump*?" Michael asks incredulously. "I'll break my fucking neck!"

Caesar shakes his head. "It's the only way. I've done it before. You just gotta tuck and roll when you hit."

"Fuck fuck fuck," Michael says. "*Fuck*."

The flashing red and blue lights get closer and closer, and Michael feels his stomach tightening. This can't be happening. Who the fuck cares if they ride a goddamn truck to Phoenix? Nobody is supposed to be out here in the first fucking place. Where the *fuck* did the cop come from?

From somewhere underneath them, there's an audible electronic *ding*, and the truck starts to slow. The angular black cop car is even closer now, so close Michael can make out its tinted windshield and gleaming chrome detail work. A shadow passes overhead, and Michael looks up out of instinct. A black octocopter zips overhead and matches speed with the police car before lowering itself back into its docking cradle on the back side of the cruiser.

"You ready?" Caesar asks. He's edging toward the side of the trailer, ready to toss his backpack over the side.

Michael nods, even though he doesn't mean it. His tongue is a sandpaper block in his mouth, and when he looks over the side of the truck at the desert rushing by, all he can picture is himself as a bloodied heap by the side of the road.

The truck is moving so slowly by now that the heat has returned, and with a vengeance. After the half hour or so they spent in the wind, the scorching sun is even worse than before.

"It's time to go, *ese*." Caesar tosses his rucksack off first, then half a second later his rifle.

"I don't know if I can—"

Michael doesn't get time to finish his sentence. Caesar jumps.

Michael scrambles over to the left side of the truck, but he can't see Caesar. His dusty white dishdasha has already blended into the dirt, and the truck continues to move. Michael grabs his backpack and readies himself, resisting the urge to throw up.

The truck shifts under his feet, and he collapses backward onto the trailer rather than allowing himself to pitch over the side. The truck slows further as it pulls off into the right shoulder. Michael contemplates jumping again before the squelch of a siren freezes him in his tracks.

The cop car has arrived, a late-model Ford in all black, save a silver *RTCSS*—Restricted Territory Contracted Security Services—down the side. The red and blue lights reflect off the white of the trailer, and Michael's life flashes before his eyes. He doesn't know what the penalty for truck-hopping is, but he knows it's probably a few months' jail time at the least, and once he goes in, he knows he'll have to start all over again when he gets out.

He should have jumped, like Caesar said. Goddamn it, where was his courage from earlier?

He stands up, preparing to make a run and leap off the right side of the trailer.

"Don't even think about it," the cop says over his car's loudspeaker. As if to emphasize the futility of such an attempt, the menacing octocopter lifts off with a buzz and hovers over the trailer. "Stay right where you are and put your hands over your head."

Michael does so, a million excuses running through his head. He'd gotten out of trouble with cops in Chicago before, but somehow, he knows that down here in the RT things are different.

The driver's side gullwing door slides up, and the cop steps out—a tall, well-built white guy in his mid-thirties with close cropped hair, black ballistic-lensed sunglasses, and a no-nonsense frown on his face. Unlike Michael and Caesar who are dressed in loose-fitting man dresses and brown boots—pretty much standard uniform for the RT—the cop is in more traditional attire. Gray fatigues under a black tactical vest, with a pistol on his right hip and a taser on his left.

The cop walks to the edge of the trailer, not taking his gaze off Michael.

Michael's knees are trembling and he can hear his heartbeat in his ears. Darkness creeps into his vision, closing on him like a tunnel, but he isn't sure if it's heat exhaustion or dehydration or fear. *Just let me go.*

For a moment, the cop says nothing. Then, with a slight flick of his eyes toward his cruiser, he says, "Dispatch, this is Two-Niner Alpha."

"This is dispatch," a male voice answers from his car speaker. "Go 'head."

"Roger. Cut my cameras and voice feed, would you? I'm going ten-seven for a bit."

The dispatcher chuckles. "Again? Fourth time today. Whatcha been up to that's gotcha so busy you need to take breaks?"

"You know how it is, dispatch. Just gotta take care of something real quick."

There's an electronic chime from somewhere in the car. "Ten-four, Two-Niner Alpha. I cut your feed and video. I always do my best work when I'm on break, you know?"

"Me too," the cop replies. His wicked grin makes Michael's breath catch in his throat.

"Dispatch out," the dispatcher says.

The cop stares at Michael. "Jump on down here, toasty," the cop says. Part of Michael is proud, for a fleeting moment, that he's been mistaken as a local.

"O-okay." Michael turns toward the rope ladder behind him.

"*Stop*," the cop says, hand on his pistol. "Where the fuck are you going?"

"I'm coming down, like you said."

"Not that way, chucklefuck," the cop says. "*This* way. I said *jump*, just like your dumbass toasty friend did back there. Speaking of which—Two-Niner UAV, go find our second suspect. Authorization one-four-eight-eight."

"Acknowledged," a computer voice says from the octocopter overhead, and it zips west down I-10 with a muted whir of rotors.

The cop stares up at Michael. "Well? Are you gonna jump down like I said, or am I gonna have to shoot your dumb ass to get you down?"

"W-what?" Michael asks, his hands still above his head. "I don't…"

"*Ten… nine…*" the cop intones, drawing his pistol.

"It's a long way down!"

"*Eight… three…*" The cop raises his pistol.

Michael's feet move before his brain has time to give any conscious instructions, and he finds himself plummeting toward the pavement.

He lands like a sack of wet shit.

A bolt of pain stabs through his right ankle, and even without looking at it, he knows it's broken. "Fuuuuuck," he whimpers through clenched teeth. Wincing, he reaches for his ankle, but a kick to his ribcage knocks the breath out of him. He rolls over on his back and looks up at the cop, who's silhouetted against the noonday sun in the shade of the trailer.

"The fuck are you doing?" the cop asks.

"My… my ankle. I think it's broken," Michael whispers.

"I don't give a fuck. I didn't tell you to move, did I?"

"N-no."

"Then don't fucking move. Jesus, you toasties are fucking dumber than a bag of hammers. *Don't. Move.*" He looks over his shoulder back at his cruiser. "Computer, release the stopped truck. Authorization one-four-eight-eight."

"Acknowledged," the computer voice says again.

The Amazon transfer truck starts rolling again with a crunch of tires against the dirt. The shade disappears when the last trailer pulls past him, leaving Michael sprawled out on the hot asphalt, baking in the sun.

Waves of nausea wash over him, but he doesn't make a move to tend to his ankle or shield his eyes. He doesn't need another kick from the cop.

The officer stands over him and bends down to retrieve his backpack. He sifts through it, then tosses it on the hood of his car. "You got any drugs on you?"

Michael shakes his head. It's actually true. This time.

The cop frowns at him. "Don't you know it's illegal to truck-hop? They're not your trucks. Hell, you're not even supposed to be out in the RT without a permit anyway. You got a permit?"

Another shake of Michael's head.

"Of course you don't, you stupid-ass toasty. So what should I do? Arrest you? You wanna get arrested?"

Michael shakes his head a third time.

The cop smiles. "Well, good. 'Cause I'm not going to. It'd be a waste of my time and your time. You'd just go back, get booked, then released, and be back out here with your stupid-ass toasty friends the next day for me to catch again tomorrow. Plus, you'd never show up to court anyway, so what's the point, right? Right?"

The cop steps on his broken ankle.

Michael screams as a supernova of agony explodes through his body. It hurts like nothing else he's ever felt before. Nothing but searing pain. That's all the world is—hurt. There's no road, no sun, no desert, no backpack, no Caesar. There is only the cop's boot, pressing hard on his already-broken ankle. Michael's vision flashes white, and he vomits up his energy bar until he dry heaves.

"Goddamn are you making a mess," the cop says as he mercifully steps off Michael's ankle. "A total fucking mess."

Michael is only dimly aware of the officer's presence as he leans over him and jerks on his canteen. The cop pulls so hard he lifts Michael's body partway off the pavement, then drops him again, shooting stars across his vision when his head hits the asphalt.

"Give it to me," the cop says.

Michael fumbles with the strap and manages to gingerly tug the canteen up his chest and over his head. He extends it with a weak arm toward the cop.

The officer takes it and unscrews the lid. "I'm gonna let you go. I will. But not until after we clean up this mess you've made." He dumps the canteen onto the asphalt, and Michael suddenly understands.

It ends here.

The cop chuckles. "I see you're finally getting it." He tosses the empty canteen back into Michael's chest. "You're free to go. I'm not gonna arrest you." He looks overhead. "Of course, it is mighty hot—computer, what's the temperature?"

"One-hundred and forty-one degrees Fahrenheit," it answers.

The officer kneels down to look at Michael. "You might want to get walking, son. I reckon you got another seventy miles or so to Phoenix, at least. I don't know where you came from, but I figure it can't be close either. Best of luck to you, toasty."

He stands with a chuckle.

"Wait," Michael rasps.

"Nope."

Michael doesn't want to—doesn't want to give the asshole the satisfaction—but he can't stop himself. His tears, his precious water, drip down to the asphalt. He drags himself to a sitting position as the cop watches, leaning against the hood of his cruiser with his arms folded.

"Go ahead. Get going," the officer says.

Michael wipes his tears on his dishdasha sleeve and grits his teeth. He tries to stand, but his ankle won't take the weight. Even the slightest pressure makes his vision grow dark. He gives it another shot before the pain collapses him back to the pavement.

He stares at the cop for a moment, then spits.

The cop laughs. "Come an hour or so from now in his heat, you'll be wishing you could lick that off the interstate, you dumb fuck."

A flash of movement catches Michael's eye, and there's a second of confusion before he realizes what's happening.

The cop never sees it coming.

The butt of Caesar's anti-drone rifle smashes against the officers's head, driving him forward to the asphalt. He tries to roll over, but Caesar is too fast. The buttstock crashes into the back of the cop's head, and Micheal watches in terrified awe as Caesar snatches the cop's pistol out of his belt.

"You all right down there?" Caesar asks Michael, anti-drone rifle in his left hand, pistol in his right. "Next time I say jump, you gonna listen, huh, *ese*?"

"Y-yeah," Michael replies, wincing in pain.

Caesar laughs. "Good, 'cause I ain't gonna pull your dumb ass out the fire again."

The cop groans and tries to roll over again, before Caesar pistol whips him. "Shut up, *la hija de puta estúpida*. I got the gun now. That'll teach you to send a drone to do a man's job. Come after Caesar with a fuckin' octocopter?" He kicks the cop.

The officer says something, but Michael is too far away and in too much pain to make it out.

"I know," Caesar replies. "I ain't trying to. I'm just gonna borrow it for a minute. You can pick it up in Phoenix." His sadistic smile gleams. "Of course, you gonna have to walk there to get it, just like you told my man Michael here. See you in hell, fucker."

Paul comes to fifteen minutes later.

His head throbs and it hurts to even think, but what worries him most is the feeling of sunburn on his exposed arms and neck. All the water he has is in his car, which those two goddamn toasties had now, cruising toward Phoenix. If he doesn't get moving and find shade quick, he's not going to make it to nightfall.

He tries to radio for help, but his radio is tied to his car and they've either cut the comms off completely or it's out of range. He calls for the octocopter, because it's got a relay that might reach dispatch, but he gets nothing.

Stupid fucking vindictive toasties.

He staggers to his feet and looks east toward Phoenix, the horizon an unbroken line of shimmering heatwaves, then back west, where the horizon is much the same.

"Fuck."

He shrugs out of his tactical vest and unbuttons his shirt. Belatedly, he realizes one of them even took his sunglasses.

Jesus Christ, when I get back to dispatch I'm going to track those two fuckers till the ends of the earth.

A distortion in the heat to the west sends his heart singing. There's a truck on the road!

Out of habit, he reaches for his eStop Stick, then realizes it too is in his car. He mutters a curse as he stares down the approaching truck, then shrugs.

Fuck it. He's seen it done by toasties a million times, and they even practiced it once or twice at the police academy. *Make yourself unmistakably visible and walk directly toward the vehicle, keeping its sensor pod(s) as much in view as possible*, he remembers the police manual saying. *Raise a sign of distress, which autopilots are required by law to acknowledge.* He strips off his shirt and swings it around his head as he walks down the highway toward the truck. *The vehicle will slow upon recognizing a human in need of assistance, and will stop if the human does not move, as required first by the Gomez-Thompson Act of 2023 and then by the Return to Safe Roads Act of 2039.*

"Hey!" Paul shouts at the approaching truck. "Hey, I need a lift or at least your radio!"

The truck is close now. It doesn't seem to be slowing down much, but then again, these things can practically stop on a dime, and they aren't programmed to stop a moment before they had to.

It honks at him twice, and he smiles.

His face falls as something else from the police manual springs to mind. *Use caution when approaching automated trucks built during the Ivanka Trump Administration (2032–2036), as their programming is not required by law to be Gomez-Thompson or Return to Safe Roads compliant.*

The 2036 Kenworth T1270's autopilot registers a disturbance at 1415L, when it strikes an unauthorized pedestrian in the eastbound lane of I-10, 112.7 kilometers—roughly seventy miles—from Phoenix.

It doesn't slow down.

David Dixon is a veteran and author living with his family in Springfield, Virginia. His debut novel, *The Damsel* was published by Kyanite Press in November 2020; his short fiction appeared in Middle West Press's *Our Best War Stories,* and in the June edition of Common Tongue Magazine.

A Stranger, Passing Through

Holly Barratt

A Stranger, Passing Through

I sit by the window hiccupping and I can't even remember a time when I didn't have hiccups. Every time I think the hiccups have stopped, and I'm about to compose myself, get up smooth myself down, brush my hair and head downstairs for breakfast, another hiccup comes and I'm right back where I started. This is my life now, I think, and it's a joke, but I'm still annoyed.

The morning sunlight is shining through the slats of the shutters. Lines of light fall on the floor, onto my lap. I feel the warmth of them cut across my throat and eyes. There's a narrow gap in between the two, and beyond them only the air outside this fourth-floor hotel suite. The shutters are held together with a little metal hook and every so often they clack-clack together in the breeze, a counter-rhythm to my hiccups. My insides jumping up my throat and back down again, unprompted.

Shutters like this are a continental thing. In England we had curtains, thick and dusty, or else with mould creeping up from the bottom. Drawn back from closed windows in pigtails. Windows shut for most of the year, the condensation rising, the rain running down them. Windows shut, doors closed, our lunches indoors, our parties indoors, our narrow city streets lined with buildings made of tight packed brick, rising up to the sky, a roof of stone or a roof of smog. Our bodies laced in with layers of tights, cardigans, coats, scarves, carrying umbrellas and bags of supplies should the weather change. Always so heavy. I always felt so hemmed in in England, enclosed in a box, weighed down by artificial warmth. I longed for travel, and I imagined these other places full of lightness, with endless space stretching out towards the sea or the mountains, to walk around in a t-shirt and bare legs, with no bags, and no contingency plan.

Yet here I am, on the inside of the shutters, viewing Italy in narrow strips of light. I would like to walk holding an umbrella now; I would like the armour of a coat and scarf to guard me against winter and to walk through streets lined with tessellated buildings. I would like to watch rain creep its way down glass and I would like to smell damp, and cold cooked meats and warm stale beer. I would like that very much.

Hiccup.

I thought here I would feel free. When I met Max and he promised to whisk me away. He said he felt hemmed in by England too. Hemmed in by bad memories. Hemmed in by stuffy attitudes, boring office jobs, and petty gossip. He loved the anonymity of travel. He said he never wanted roots. Never wanted to be stuck. Changing and shifting everywhere he went. Always a stranger. I wanted that too. I wanted for us to be strangers together.

Hiccup

But the Mediterranean summer is too hot. Sun imprisons you here like rain does in England. You sit in your air-conditioned room breathing in what you just breathed out. Air cycling through your body again and again. I don't speak the language, and when I try a few halting words, the natives sigh, shake their heads, switch to English to sell me my meal or my bus ticket, complete our business with a fixed smile and a polite "Madame". Then they turn to Max, switch back to Italian, and their faces start to move again. Sometimes the men call out to me "Ciao Bella", "you want to come for a drink?" then they chatter to each other in Italian and I don't know whether I'm a goddess, a whore or a hag to them. Only that I am on the outside. A visitor. Passing through.

"Speak to me in Italian," I said to him "How can I ever learn if no-one will talk to me?"

"We'll not be here forever," he said "There's no point learning Italian, they don't speak it anywhere but Italy. French would be better. Or Spanish even."

"Then teach me French."

"I'm not a good teacher. You can learn when we get there. Take proper lessons."

But now I am in Italy and hemmed in by my Englishness. Max was fluent in three languages. Two different passports. Work he could do from anywhere. How can a man like that be hemmed in by anything? By memories, he says. He's an unlucky man. An unhappy man. I was his happy ever after. The light at the end of his tunnel.

I said "I don't want to be the light at the end of your tunnel. I want to walk with you through the dark."

He said "nothing is dark with you around. I'm happy now. We're happy. We're free."

Hiccup.

I am not drunk. The last drink I had was one that Max brought me, as he did, every day, every evening, sitting at this window with the shutters clacking. Only one drink. A brandy and lemonade. I prefer beer. Beer isn't ladylike and gives you gas. Well, here I am with hiccups anyway.

I don't remember how long I've been here. I remember other things but they seem so distant and small. Sitting on a plane, checking into a hotel, drinking a cappuccino and Max telling me that milky coffee should only be drunk before lunch – all those things seem like childhood memories even though they can't have been a month ago? A week ago? An hour ago? I can't imagine what it's like to not have hiccups. I can't remember what the room looks like behind me.

These lines of light and warmth. They haven't moved. They should have travelled down my body, narrowing as the sun gets higher. Perhaps I haven't been sitting here as long as I imagined. But that click-clack of the shutters: it's the exact same click-clack each time. I watch it, the left shutter moves out slightly, pulls on the hook, the right one follows, then they're pulled back and clack together. Then I hiccup. Then the breeze again, cuts through the warmth, then the left shutter moves, then the right, then they clack, then I hiccup. Then the breeze. And I notice the church bell in the distance – the same flat sound, again and again. It should be striking the quarter hour, the half hour, the next hour – but it doesn't. Everything repeats. It's the same. How long have I been here? The stripe on my brow and across my wrist warming. My thighs close together, my right hand in my lap with my thumb just touching the first finger like that. Hiccupping the same hiccup. Breathing the same breath. Have I even blinked?

And then I decide to move. It's all I need to do. To decide. I move my thumb away from my finger. I straighten my back. I lift a hand to my face. One-two-three.

And I don't hiccup.

And the bells don't ring and click-clack of the shutters changes its rhythm. The stripes of warmth fall down my body to the floor and my face feels cold. My body feels cold, but still. I feel no draft, no breeze, no movement. I see the breeze. Hear the breeze. But I don't feel it on my skin. I twist my body to the bedside table. My hairbrush is not where I left it. My fingers brush the bedside table but feel nothing. There is a novel in French. I feel light as ash. There is a glass with the water from melted ice at the bottom.

I remember the brandy and lemonade. I was standing by the window. Did I put down the glass? There? Anywhere? I was standing by the window. The shutters were open. Banging against the wall. I had hiccups. I always get hiccups, after a drink. After Max's drinks. I was lighter than ash. Then heavy as an asteroid. Falling. I remember falling. I can't handle my drink. I was homesick. I drank too much. I was unlucky. Max was unlucky.

To lose one wife might be considered a misfortune. To lose two?

I pull myself upwards, it feels more like floating than standing. Like in yoga when they say make the body light. I spin. The room behind me is unfamiliar. The shape is the same. My hairbrush is not there. The bedclothes are different. When were those changed? There is make up scattered across the dressing table. Something yellow draped over a chair. I could never wear yellow. It doesn't work with my skin tone. These are another woman's things. I know it before she enters.

She has fashionable blonde hair, a French braid that I never had the patience for, a subtle streak of violet. She wears red lipstick. A deep blue satin blouse, half tucked into loose jeans. It all speaks of relaxed chic, but her eyes are wide, her red lips pressed together, she fiddles with a gold stud earring, twizzling it and twizzling it. She sits down on the chair as Max follows her in. Neither of them see me. I am not really here.

Max is anxious too. His shirt sleeves are rolled up, and there's a wet patch spreading across his chest. I remember the smell of that, sweat when fresh and just cooked by sun. He scrapes a hand through his hair. It's longer now, still shiny and black, with flecks of white just above the ears. I remember it felt like lametta on a Christmas tree, running my hands through it. How can it feel so silky without conditioner? I asked him. I'm so jealous of your hair.

"All women are jealous of my hair," he said, and his hands were on my waist and he was kissing me. And I thought I could smell Italy on his skin. I thought I could smell the world.

"Do you think…" he says to the woman he can see. "I know, I hate asking this."

He walks over and kneels by her side, and his hand is on her waist.

"Perhaps you could ask your father for a loan? Just for the last little bit? I'm good for the rest, you know that – but if Garcia can't pay me until next month we'll miss out. I really want to be able to take you to Guadeloupe."

The woman says something in French. I haven't spoken French since my D-grade GCSE, but I know it when I hear it. Max speaks French back to her. Then they switch to English.

"OK, sure, I can ask. But after I pay him back that's the last of it. I told you Max I really want to sever that connection. I'm never going back."

Her accent isn't French. It might be American. Maybe Canadian. Perhaps even Irish. I don't know. I'm not good with accents, I would have got better, if I travelled more. She raises her hand and runs it through his hair. I can almost feel the silk black strands on the skin of her fingers.

"I can't believe you never use conditioner," she says. "I think you're a liar."

"Never," he says. "Could I ever look into those big blue eyes and tell a lie?"

He touches noses with her. Eskimo kiss. Then plants his lips on hers. Wipes his mouth.

"You don't need the lipstick you know." Your lips are already beautiful. "And the people around here are traditional, they associate obvious make up with…"

"Whores?"

"A certain kind of woman. I know that's not you, but they don't."

"But what if I am Max?," she says, her hands on his wrists. "What if I have the spirit of a whore? What if I like the idea of being a courtesan, with men in her thrall? What if it sounds like freedom?"

He laughs, in his speaking voice. Not his real laugh.

"Oh you're sweet," he says. "But I know you Lili. You dress trendy, you talk tough, but you're full of nothing but love. Your heart is so big and you've been searching. You've always been so alone, and looking for someone to love and now you have me."

"I wasn't always alone."

"You were. Your soul was alone. Spiritually alone – until I found you. And so was I. When my wife died I thought I would never find love again. I was lost. Empty. But you saved me Lili. We saved each other."

She looks over her shoulder, and I think, for a moment, that she sees me. I look into her eyes, so blue they're almost navy. She is beautiful. A little younger than me. Not by much.

"What is it?"

"Nothing, nothing, just the wind."

They slip back into French, or Franglais. I only catch every other word. Then he pushes her back on the bed. Her hands slip around his waist, up to his shoulders, she lifts him off her to unbutton his shirt. No Lili, no, he likes to do that himself. Or to leave it on. You can't know that yet. He moves her hands away and kisses her, pushes her back down. I watch them make love in the room that used to be mine. I have been erased. A straight line of history now, an emptiness of Max from the death of his wife in the England he couldn't bear, to Lili here today. I was never here.

Unless I am the wife. We never married, but maybe I am the dead wife in this story. Maybe he wasn't married to the wife in the story he told me either. Maybe there was no wife. Maybe there were many wives. When I fell what happened? When my body hit the ground outside. What then? I came to sit by the window with my hiccups, but what was happening outside this room? Did I go to hospital? Did I die on the cobblestones? Am I even dead? Am I still sleeping, anonymous in some Italian hospital, named or unnamed. Does Max visit me? Did anyone know I was here with him? Am I buried? Did I burn? Was there a funeral? Was it written up in the newspaper as a terrible accident? A mysterious disappearance? Am I in some unmarked grave beyond the city? Am I under water? In a forest? Was I ever here? Or did I pass through, unnoticed, a stranger, light as ash?

When they finish he gets up immediately. She gathers the sheets around her. He buttons his trousers and smooths his hair. He looks at the clock. He leaves the room then comes back with a drink. Two glasses with sparkling liquid, on clear one cloudy – brandy and lemonade. This, at least is the same. He puts the cloudy glass down beside her, strokes her cheek with the back of his knuckle. His hands are rough as a cat's tongue, although the rest of him is smooth. He sits back and watches her as he sips on his clear liquid. She drinks, she starts to talk to him in French again. He answers in monosyllables. He is scrolling through his phone. He stands up, he gives her a kiss, and he leaves the room. She sits up, the duvet gathered at her chest covering her breasts even though she doesn't know anyone can see her. She drains the last of the drink.

She hiccups.

Her flesh is creamy pale. In Italy at this time of year, she ought to be browned or burned. Her skin speaks of the inside of rooms and closed top cars, of recycled air, of sitting still and waiting. Waiting like Penelope waited for Odysseus, dutifully weaving and unweaving the same threads.

She reaches through me. Her arm passes right through. I don't feel a thing. She unhooks the shutters and lets them swing open, crashing against the walls. She gets up and attaches them to the hooks on the walls either side. I did this too. A drunk or suicidal woman does not hook the shutters onto the walls. She sits back on the bed and closes her eyes, lets the breeze I can't feel come into the room, cut through the sticky post-sex sweat. Then she stands up and walks to the window, looks out at the street. I look with her. It's a long time since I saw the street. Or any street.

Peach and peppermint coloured buildings, with bubbles of peeling paint. Twisted iron rails on balconies. Silk knickers fluttering on lines. A policeman on a moped, winding his way around parked cars. A group of young men, brown arms in short sleeved white shirts, arguing or just chatting. Two laughing women with ice-creams and backpacks. A skinny cat curls around a doorway then disappears. One of the men looks up, sees her: bare shouldered and smudge-lipped standing in the open window.

"Ciao Bella!" he shouts

She shrugs a shoulder, blows a kiss

"Ciao!"

Then she withdraws back into the room. Shuts the shutters again. She hiccups again. And swears. And holds her breath. Trying to get rid of them that way, I suppose. I see her future laid out before me. I don't know if she still imagines she will see Guadaloupe, or France, or England, or anywhere else. I don't know if she thinks she will see any more of Italy again other than what lies just outside this window, where she is framed like a painting. I don't know if she'll fall. Or if she'll jump. Or if he'll push her. If the drinks don't do the trick he'll have to push. Maybe he intends to keep her, for her beautiful shoulders, or her father's money, or maybe his plan is always to kill us. But she could still escape. She's still alive. She can still throw the shutters open and feel the breeze and flirt with boys.

If I'd done that. If I'd been braver. If I hadn't drunk so much. If I'd walked away. If I'd been less in love. Less naïve. If I'd had less faith that things would get better. If his hair was less silky. I could leave this room. I could travel for real. I could be free to go anywhere. Like she is.

I wonder if. I wonder if I still could? Can myself slip inside her? Can I walk away? Could I live in this body, now mine is lost somewhere? This slim waist, this soft skin? Could I slip it on like a blue silk blouse and with a new beauty, a new daring, walk away?

I kneel in front of her. I focus on her eyes, her lips. I am light, but there is a force within me. A determination. If you can dream it you can be it. Don't dream it, be it. Was that from a film? Or just some cheesy fridge magnet. I push my lightness into the space she occupies. I feel myself filling her out.

I think of yoga classes again. Meditations. The teacher saying "Imagine a light entering your body and spreading out down every limb, every nerve, every blood vessel."

I am the light. I spread out around her neck over the top of her head around her eyes, down each arm into the tip of each finger. She breathes me in and I fill up her belly, her diaphragm.

No more hiccups. I am the light and I'm here to calm you.

In my own time I flicker my eyes open, reborn. It's no different looking through blue eyes than it is through brown ones. I look around at the room, from inside my new body. I raise a hand up through the air. The air has weight. It's sticky and slow. The breeze is pointed and fresh as lemon zest. I run a hand over my new right thigh. It's slightly stubbled with spikes of dark hair. The blonde isn't natural then.

There is not much time. I open drawers and throw on clothes. Shorts, a long-sleeved kaftan, a baseball cap, sunglasses. I look around for a handbag. I find only a tiny clutch on the dresser, with a lipstick and some tampons, and an empty folded tote from some museum. I go to Max's side of the bed with the little chest of drawers. I tip it forward. The front of the draws is thick and I don't know how to pick a lock, but the back of the cabinet is shoddy MDF. He wouldn't expect so much violence from either of us, but dead women know what it takes. We don't hang about. With a pair of nail scissors I stab at the flimsy wood until a hole forms, and then I tear strips off until I'm inside. There's cash in envelopes. Different currencies. I stuff it all into the museum tote. A blue cardboard folder – passports – my own, faded with a picture of my face six years ago, young and blank as a ghost. Useless now, but I take it anyway. Then hers – it turns out she's Swiss, which surprises me. I wonder if I can speak French now. Does language sit in the body? Do I have any others?

I take her passport. It's a shame Max's isn't here or I would take that too. I do find an assortment of other passports, mostly for women, but a few for men – the male ones have pictures of Max at different ages, with different names. I take those. I also take the credit cards I find. I might not be able to use them, but why make it easy for him to come after us?

We leave the room. I run her down the stairs. It feels like driving a car, although it's a long time since I did that, I'm in control but the parameters of what I'm controlling aren't quite part of me. I feel the slap of her sandals on each step as a distant sensation. It's like virtual reality. I hear our breathing quick and sharp, the flutter of a foreign heart in my chest, praying Max will not be coming the other way, thinking of an excuse, a run to the shop, something dropped from the window? When my voice comes out who will he hear? Me or her?

We make it down the empty stairwell, I throw open the door, and the world hits me in the face like a steam oven. It's still afternoon and the sun is bright through my sunglasses. It's a world I haven't seen for a long time. A country I never got to see properly, but I must resist the urge to delay. I can always come back one day. If I can just escape now, I can go wherever I like, forever. When this body dies, I can jump to a new one, a new one after that, keep going, keep living, forever.

Just run. Don't look too suspicious. Slow down. Don't look anxious. Don't draw attention. Don't look around too much but stay aware. Cross the road to avoid that group of men. Hunch. Don't look beautiful. But don't look vulnerable either. Look like you know where you're headed. Walk like you own the street.

"Ciao Bella!"

Not that much.

I turn corners, and corners and corners. I don't know where I'm going yet. I just need to get far away from where Max thinks I am. Buy some time. I find a crowd. Tourists. A cacophony of languages. Smells of panini, gelato, sunscreen and sweat. I spot a paper map, dropped on the ground, pick it up and examine it. I stand next to four chattering women around my age, trying to look like part of their group, as I try and remember the shape of the streets I've run along to get here, get a sense of my location, somewhere I might find an airport bus or a train station.

"Hiccup"

Something inside me. My diaphragm moves.

"Look up."

I don't want to look up. My face might be seen. But the command comes from inside.

"Lookup"

She's still here. I've pushed her back, but she's still there in the pit of my stomach. We're in this body together, and I'm not sure I'm welcome but maybe she wants to get away as much as I do. We can fight for control later.

I look up. And there's what I wanted, from Rome.

Towering above me, all the Gods with their beautiful curled beards. The muscled thighs and chests. The water running over beautiful waving hair, over muscles that seemed to flex in the light. They say the devil is a handsome man, but the Gods aren't half bad either. Our stomach somersaults. I feel the familiar flush of hormones, warming through all my limbs, tickling at the underside of my skin. I feel like a teenager again, watching a boyband, shirts ripped off, strategically hosed down for the video. Oh, Max is this why you didn't want me here? You aren't the only man with beautiful hair!

I came here to Italy and then never saw the Trevi Fountain until now. None of those bucket list things I was seeking. I was here months and Max always said he would bring me here one day. When the weather was good. When it wasn't tourist season. When he wasn't busy. No it wasn't safe to go alone. Italian men are predators. Especially on naïve young British girls.

"I'm not naïve," I said

I was. I didn't want to be. And I thought coming to Italy would make me less so. Eventually it worked. I tear my gaze from the chiselled abs. No time for men. No time for sex. No time for sightseeing of any kind not now, not yet. One day soon. A train seems sensible. It will be harder to escape, if he does happen to catch me. But there are more places to hide. I trace the streets to the nearest metro station. The map tells me a train to the airport. I set off, it's just a five minute walk, then I can duck underground. Weave through the crowds. Then run up against the turnstiles. I don't know how to buy a ticket. I don't know which ticket I need. Or how to use it. I should have bought a guide book somewhere. An Idiot's Guide to Italy or something. Slipped into a tourist shop. There are instructions in English on the machine but I can't make sense of them. The only train tickets I ever bought were in England, where I walked up to a desk in a town centre station and told them where I wanted to be. But this is Europe, right? The transport system crosses borders, it must be similar country to country. And easier, if you speak some of the language. Swiss people are renowned for being good linguists right? She spoke French, but maybe she speaks Italian too?

I bend over in the corner so my head is down, I pretend to fiddle with my bag. I close my eyes. I turn myself inwards.

"Lili?" I try and say it down into my diaphragm. For some reason that's where I feel she is. A trapped breath. "Lilli. Are you still here?"

I wait. I try to quiet my mind like in the meditation sessions I went to long ago searching for inner peace. Let your mind be like a still pool into which the universe can drop stones of wisdom. Lili drop a pebble. The water ripples. It hisses like the wind.

"Get the hell out of my body bitch."

"No, shhsh, Lili, I'm sorry…"

"Get out. I don't know who you are buit…"

"Lili, I'm sorry. I should have asked permission. I didn't know how."

"This body is mine. You can't have it."

"But Max can?"

"What?"

"Max. He tries to tell you what to do. He tries to keep you in that hotel room. He tries to tell you what to wear."

"I do whatever I like. I travel with him. He's not my keeper."

"Is that true? Were you going to ask your father for money like he asked?"

"For us. For our future. My Dad has plenty of money."

"Is it your future though? Or is just his? That business venture – do you even know what it is? Do you even know what he does?"

"I don't need to know…" she sounds less certain.

"He had your passport and credit cards locked up in a safe. Did you have the key?"

I feel her flip over in my belly

"You were there. You saw all of those passports. You saw mine. See?" I get my passport out of the bag, hold my picture, my name up to our eyes. "That's me. He took my passport. He took my money. He persuaded me it wasn't safe to go out. He stopped me learning Italian. He promised to show me the world and I spent months trapped in a tiny apartment. He gave me a drink that made me sleepy and lethargic, then one day I fell out of the window. Maybe he even pushed me. And what do you think happened to those other women in those other passport pictures? Did he tell you about his dead wife? How many dead wives do you think there are?"

"The drinks?"

"Yes. That's what made you hiccup. Made your brain foggy. Tell me you didn't used to feel more alive before you came here?"

"You can't have my body. This is mine. I'm sorry for what happened, but this is mine."

"I need you Lili. We need to work together. I've got you out of the apartment before it was too late. By the time you realised yourself you would have been too far gone. But now I need your help. I don't know how to buy a train ticket. I don't speak Italian. Can you help? Get us to the airport. We'll fly to England together, get beyond his reach – then I'll find a way out of this I promise. We just need to ride together a while, and we need to do it fast. He might already realise we're gone."

"OK. OK. Be quiet then. Give me my brain back."

I don't know quite what to do, but I try to curl up into a ball of what's left of me. I settle into the back of her brain, with just one soul-eye poking out watching what she's doing through a tiny hole, a periscope. It's like watching a film, in a foreign language, on a shitty TV, with a terrible signal. And my hands tied behind my back. At least I know what's happening. At least I consented to it.

"Sorry I didn't warn you before I took over." I whispered to her.

"Shush."

Her fingers skim over the various buttons of the ticket machine. I notice she uses the French language setting, so that must be her mother tongue. I'm glad it's not English – if we're both going to be living here then there's no point us having the same default language. She smoothly walks through the turnstiles, apologises in Italian to someone she brushes a little too close to. She boards the train, stays standing even though there are seats available. That's good, she knows she needs to be able to see up and down the carriage, to be able to move quickly. She swings off the train when it reaches the airport, heads to the departures board to look for flights leaving in a few hours. Something with time still to buy tickets but that won't leave us hanging around. If I stay still, if I try and calm my mind and get receptive, I can hear her thoughts. I can feel they're in French, but because I'm inside I can recognise the gist of them, watch them, more like pictures or sensations. There are a lot of possible destinations.

"It needs to be Europe. Somewhere where I won't need a visa, where I can just enter. France."

"No. He knows you'll be comfortable there. Nowhere French speaking. Not for now. And not Switzerland either."

"Ha. Over my dead body. Erm – sorry. Where then?"

"England."

"Really?" I feel her wrinkle our nose.

I hate England as much as anyone but her disgust offends me.

"I have a flat there. Max persuaded me to rent it out so we could travel on the income. With any luck it's still in my name. The rent went to our joint bank account but it was in my name. And we never married so it won't have been easy for him to take ownership. We can sell it. Then we can run wherever we like with that money."

"We? You think you're staying in my body?"

"You want to go back to your Daddy for money?"

"I'll get a job."

I uncurl, I grow myself big, stretch out so I fill her up completely. Then I walk over to the vending machine, buy a can of cola, shake it up, open it and let the liquid fizz all over that nice blue shirt and jeans. Then I shrink back down, just a little.

"You bitch!"

A few people turn around to look.

"Stop drawing attention to us."

"You can talk."

"Look. I'm on your side. I wanted to rescue you. I didn't want to see another woman fall out of that window. I don't want Max to keep doing this. But I don't want to stay dead either. He's not going to do that to me any more than he's going to do it to you. So we're going to have to come to some arrangement. Alternate days, whatever. I don't care, but I'm here now and I'm not going to leave you alone."

She's on her phone, buying a ticket to Heathrow. She almost buys two.

"I can't deal with you being in my body with me."

"I can stay quiet. On your days I'll just curl up. Leave you in peace."

"I'll know you're there. When I'm peeing."

"That's what you're worried about?"

"Not exclusively no. I get it. You don't want to die. I can sympathise. But this body is occupied. In use. We need to get you a new one."

"A new one? How…"

"Would you object to being a man?"

I've thought about it often. The freedom to walk down streets at night, to sit with my legs apart on buses, to drink alone in bars, to not bleed every month for half my life. I wouldn't mind giving it a try.

"Go on?"

"How about we head back to the city? How about we send Max out of that window. How about at the crucial moment you enter his body? And you get to do whatever you like with it?"

I imagine it. Having that soft skin, and silky hair, all for myself, all for my own.

"Deal."

Holly Barratt *is a writer living in Wales who primarily writes short stories in the science fiction, horror and magic realism genres. We first published her in our Call of the Wyld anthology (available now from bookshops, from Amazon or our website www.wyldblood.com). She is currently working on a novel.*

Final Exam, Demonology
Karl Dandenell

Final Exam, Demonology

"Do I *have* to dismiss the demon?" said Sugyen. The apprentice stared at the fearsome creature imprisoned within the circle of blood runes and flickering candles. "It feels cruel, dragging the poor thing here just to send it back straight away."

Ymir, his master, shook his head. "Any apprentice can *summon* a demon. Only a full wizard can *control* and *dismiss*. Now get on with it."

"Yes, please hurry," said the demon. "I'm in complete agony over here."

"No one asked you, Gwal'laghamandar!" snapped Ymir. He whispered a few syllables. Blisters rose on the demon's back.

Gwal'laghamandar hissed in pain.

Ymir lowered his voice. "Look, Sugyen, you're an excellent student. But your priorities are all wrong. You need to spend *less* time caring for every injured toad and vole that crosses your path and *more* time learning the finer elements of the magical arts."

"Like demon control," said Sugyen.

"Precisely!" said Ymir, happy that Sugyen agreed with him. "The first time I summoned a demon, I was so scared I nearly wet myself. But once I realized I had the thing under my control, well, I *knew* I would become a great wizard and do great things."

Sugyen nodded. "Like getting this keep. I know." As a young wizard, Ymir had summoned up a relatively minor demon, then tasked it with procuring fifteen perfect emeralds from the black dragon Enok the Terrible. Those gems had paid for and furnished Ymir's keep, including an extensive orchard of rare fruit trees. Ymir had regaled Sugyen with the story on his first night as an apprentice. And repeatedly thereafter.

"Pity the demon didn't think to *kill* the dragon before taking the emeralds," said Ymir.

"So you summoned *another* demon—"

"Exactly," said Ymir. "*That* demon handled the foul lizard after it torched my beautiful orchard. Quite the battle, let me tell you."

"Master," said Sugyen, hoping to forestall another reminiscence. "Why didn't you just order the first demon to kill the dragon? You taught me demons are impervious to dragon fire."

"Indeed. The physical forms of demons are nearly impossible to kill in this realm," said Ymir. "Only their true names combined with certain magics can affect them."

"Then—oh, right." Sugyen blushed. "Service or Saga."

"I glad you remember *some* of your demonic theory," said Ymir, his voice falling into a familiar teaching rhythm. "Once a demon performs physical labor for you—successfully—it's free to go, and you can't summon it a second time. On the *other* hand, if the demon only answers questions…?"

"Then you can call upon it as often as needed," finished Sugyen. "Hardly seems fair, given the painful nature of summoning."

"Demons barely notice. Trust me." Ymir pulled out two scrolls. "Now then—here are your spells: *Total Demonic Control* and *Immediate Demonic Dismissal*. Once you've sent Gwal'laghamandar back to his realm, I'll consider your apprenticeship complete." He handed over the scrolls.

"I'm going to down to the cellar and find a nice brandy to celebrate. You two play nice, now." Ymir closed the heavy door behind him.

Sugyen recited the spell of Total Demonic Control, taking special care with his pronunciation. Once the spell was cast, the demon sighed and scratched its belly with a black, serrated talon. "What is thy bidding?"

Sugyen opened the second scroll, then paused, thinking to indulge his curiosity. "I bid you answer truthfully, Gwal'laghamandar. Does it truly pain you when you are summoned?"

"Does it pain me? Imagine being crushed to death between two millstones, over and over," said the demon. "Now give me a task, Master, so I may depart and never see you again."

Sugyen had been so worried about performing his spells he hadn't thought about a task. "Uh, I have no labor for you. Only questions."

"Just like the others." Gwal'laghamandar narrowed its eyes. "Of Ymir's eight apprentices, only two have allowed me to fulfill my contract. The remainder hold me in thrall, summoning me whenever they seek some trivial bit of arcane knowledge."

"But I wouldn't do that," said Sugyen. "I hate seeing things suffer. Ask anyone! Honestly, now that I know the truth, I couldn't see myself ever summoning you again."

"Eventually, you will summon me. That's what wizards *do*."

Sugyen considered all the animals he'd nursed back to health. As much as he wanted to keep them as pets, he always released them, knowing they could only thrive in their natural habitats. Was it not reasonable to think demons, too, required such treatment?

Then he remembered Ymir's comment about demonic theory. "You know, there might be a way to keep you safe from another summoning."

"How?"

"I could bestow a new name on you."

Gwal'laghamandar shook its head. "I know wizards can name things, but it makes no difference. Whatever name you give me will be shared, and I'll find myself right back here. Suffering."

"Not if I don't remember the name." Sugyen sketched out his plan.

"I have my doubts," said the demon, "though I cannot see any good alternative given my circumstances. Proceed, wizardling."

Sugyen opened the chamber door, took a deep breath, and placed his left hand in the frame. "Do you, Gwal'laghamandar, accept a new name to bind you both body and spirit?"

"I do."

"Then I name you—" Sugyen slammed the door, crushing his fingers. He shrieked and cursed, jumping about the chamber.

Gwal'laghamandar laughed. "A most excellent name. I will bear it with pride."

"Glad you like it." Sugyen wheezed with pain.

"Now task me so I can depart. Hurry! Ymir approaches."

Sugyen looked around, shaking his fingers. "I, uh, command you to remove the cobwebs from the ceiling!" That seemed safe enough.

"Done." The candles in the summoning circle flared, scouring the ceiling. When the flames died down, Gwal'laghamandar disappeared, his contract fulfilled.

A moment later, Ymir stepped into the room with a bottle and two goblets. "I heard screaming. Everything all right?"

"Fine, master. Just had to remind the demon who was in charge."

"Good, good. I'm glad to see you're starting to act like a proper wizard." The old wizard filled the goblets with brandy. "A toast to your first demon!"

"My first demon!" said Sugyen, his hand throbbing. *And hopefully my last.*

Karl Dandenell *is a graduate of Viable Paradise and a Full Member of the Science Fiction Writers of America. He and his family, plus their cat overlords, live on an island near San Francisco famous for its Victorian architecture and low-speed traffic. Karl's preferred drinks are strong Swedish tea and single-malt whiskey and he posts randomly on his blog (www.firewombats.com) and Twitter (@kdandenell).*

Vanishing Ink

Adam Breckenridge

Vanishing Ink

Sometimes I just want to rip the curtains open and let all the devils scratching at the glass outside gaze upon me, let their weird eyes do what they will. But most days my curiosity never goes beyond the cautious peeks I steal through the edges of the curtains, at claws and black bits of flesh that press against the glass, leaving not so much as a crack for the empty depths behind them to darken through. I do this daily, though I dread the sight of them, dread the occasions that I spot a face sneering at me, which is enough to leave me so shaken that I find myself huddling for hours in the center of the room. Their faces are a terror to behold, so vicious and empty at the same time, like a well of poisoned air.

When I was a child the claws scratching on the glass were just tree branches, so harmless by day but by night I was certain it was their intention to smash through the window and crush me in their grip. I remember running to my parent's bedroom in the night, weeping into their pajamas while they laughed away my anxieties.

"Shall I chop the trees down and pulp them into stationary for our store?" my father would ask.

But they were so beautiful by day, growing up through the concrete to surround our shop, protecting us with their shadows. I thought the wind rustling the leaves were conversations they carried on above me. I wanted to climb them so I could hear what they said and maybe talk to them myself, try to convince them to protect me at night, but their lowest branches were well beyond my reach.

The trees are long gone, as is the sidewalk around the shop that they grew from. There is nothing left but me, the demons outside who endlessly taunt me, and the shop, with its thousands of jars of ink my parents left behind.

People used to come for miles to buy the ink my parents sold, because no matter what you needed it for, ours was always the best. Our apple ink produced fuller apples than anyone else's, if one needed to repair a leaky roof our patching ink could fill in a hole that would outlast the plaster around it, for a leisurely weekend our breeze ink drew a soft wind that coupled well with the shade you could draw to lie in.

Most of these inks serve no function now, as they would need some substance outside of the bounds of the shop to be of any use. What good is ink for drawing tulips when there is no light for them, or ink for drawing locks when there is no one to keep out, or even ink for calligraphy, when there is no one to admire your penmanship?

It was with the most childish of inks that my parents managed to save us from the nothing. Vanishing ink sold for pennies a pint and once you matured past the age of seven you could only turn your nose up at any kid still naïve enough to be delighted by its trickery, though it is a wondrous thing the first time your mother draws a line on a sheet of paper for you and then inches her fingers towards it until they cross the line and disappear. Carefully she would wait just long enough for your astonishment to register before shoving her whole arm across, a clean slice across her arm precisely where the line was drawn. Then quickly, lest your amazement grow to alarm, she pulled it back to show that it's still intact.

I remember spending hours with my first well of vanishing ink, drawing a line on a sheet of paper as my mother had done and experimenting with sticking my arm across quickly and slowly, waving it back and forth, hoping to shake loose the mystery of its function. Every child, after awhile, gives in to the temptation to stick their head across the line and see what happens, and every child learns then that their head is still there, just not visible to others. This leads inevitably to the first time you draw a line of ink on the ground and jump across it, only to learn that the ink doesn't work more than a few inches above the line you drew and that when you land you will at most find yourself standing on invisible feet and that even if you keep them invisible, the effect wears off after a few minutes.

Thus every child grows weary of vanishing ink quickly after the disappointing limitations of the substance are revealed. And so I couldn't help but groan when I came downstairs into the shop to find my mother playing with it, sticking her arm across and pulling it back out.

"Mom, what are you doing?" I asked, "that stuff is for babies."

"I'm thinking about nothing," she said, and I understood what she meant.

My mother, like so many others, had been increasingly bogged down by worries over the growing patches of nothingness that were emerging around the world. It was not the first time we had had problems with nothingness. Like thunderstorms or solar flares, occasional bursts of nothingness would appear and vanish as quickly as they had come. It was treated the same way as any other disaster, with police cordoning off the patches until they faded away and warnings on the news of increased activity of nothingness. I even saw a patch of nothing once, when I was out playing with friends.

It's hard to say how big it was, since the size of a patch of nothing is difficult to determine, but it was relatively small and, like all nothing, lacking in color, which is impossible to describe unless you've seen it. We had fun throwing rocks and sticks at it, dared each other to jump in, though none of us ever would have done it, as it would have meant that we'd cease to exist.

But no one had ever seen anything like this new kind of nothing before. Not only were patches appearing and not fading away, word was the patches were growing and expanding too. Some people even spoke of entire towns being swallowed up by it, though it only seemed to happen in places far away. No one knew what to make of it.

So I understood what she meant by nothing. What I did not understand was what vanishing ink had to do with nothingness.

I gave it no more thought until a few weeks later. My mind had been too much elsewhere. The stories of the nothing were getting worse: the patches were growing bigger and getting closer, close enough that the stories weren't so easily dismissible now. People we trusted had come in to tell us they'd seen it for themselves, that this was like no nothing that had ever come before. Some were planning to flee, everyone was on edge, which is what made it so strange when I came down from my room and I saw mom and dad in the back room playing with vanishing ink again.

"Are you guys seriously still playing with that stuff?" I asked as I approached them, then reached out my arm towards the line they had drawn on the tabletop.

"Don't," my mother screamed and batted my arm away. I jumped back, my heart racing. She had never yelled at me before.

"What was that about?"

My dad spoke up.

"This isn't the usual vanishing ink son," he said, "we've made a special batch of it, like nothing anyone has made before. Watch."

He went to the refrigerator, rummaged for a minute, then came back with a carrot. Carefully he nudged the carrot point first across the line and it vanished as you would expect. When it was halfway across he stopped and pulled it back. But while I was expecting it to re-emerge fully intact, instead it was still half missing.

"Anything that vanishes across this line vanishes for good," my mom said, "it doesn't just make it look like nothing is there, there really is nothing there."

I stared at them in confusion.

"But who's gonna want to buy an ink that does that?"

They looked at each other.

"This isn't to sell, son," my dad said, "it's to protect us from the nothing."

Again, I understood what he meant. But how vanishing ink, no matter how it was modified, could help us was beyond me.

"You still haven't figured it out?" my mom asked after a moment of silence. She continued before I could answer. "The ink, if we made it right, works both ways. Not only will it turn something into nothing, it also turns nothing into something."

"But what will it turn into?" I asked.

"There's no way to know," she said, "it could literally be anything, but what's important is that it won't be nothing. Nothing is absolute, there's, well, nothing we can do to stop it, but if we can turn it into something tangible we can face it, find a way to stop it. This gives us at least a little cause for hope."

Not much, as we would find out. I thought I had finally worked up the nerve to talk about it, but I guess its still too tender for me. My parents died protecting these inks from the plagues, the riots, the fires and the hunger of the darkness and every other evil thing that came down upon us as the nothing took over. Sometimes I think the nothing might have been better.

My wells of ink for drawing food have been running dry, and there are few things more frustrating than to crave an apple only to find halfway through drawing one that you only have enough ink for a core. Retrieving more ink, woefully, meant having to descend down into the shop to face naked the eyes of the demons who gather round the windows down there as I fumbled around among the thousands of jars of ink that my parents had never bothered to label. There have been times when I starved for days rather than face them because I needed the imminent threat of death to inspire me to confront them.

This time though I had a new plan to take as much time as I needed for as many inks as I needed without having to fear their gaze. During one of my searches for ink to make food I stumbled across ink that could draw masks. I had forgotten we had it, though it had always been so popular during Halloween that my parents could barely mix it fast enough. My dad always had to draw my masks for me, because I could never handle the ink well enough myself to draw anything other than crude pseudo-faces.

At the time I couldn't see any practical use for the ink, but, because I found myself tearing up for the nostalgia it brought me, I took some back upstairs with me. I'm grateful now I did, because it gave me an inspiration. My hand is much steadier than it used to be, and I find now that I am able to draw a passable demon mask. Perhaps I could make them think I was one of them. Maybe I would even start to believe, just a little bit, that I was one of them too, and I would have less cause to fear them.

It was terrifying to step into the gaze of the demons who pressed against the window, though I tried my best to move like them, wisp-like and fluid, as though I might vanish into the shadows at any moment. I found it impossible, however, to resist breaking away from my dance and running my finger against the hilt of the sword I always carried with me when I went downstairs. It seemed my ruse was working – the demons weren't cackling as they are wont to do – there was no rattling of the glass, no scratching of claws, but some of them imitated my movements as I undulated my limbs and body across the floor, snickering to themselves.

Just as I was about to enter the storeroom, I turned to look at them one more time and saw the leering face of one of them standing inches from mine. I was so startled by its unexpected appearance that, without thinking, I unsheathed my sword and cut its laughing head off. The head splattered when it hit the floor, forming a stain of ink in the shape of its face that began to eat through the wood, leaving only the impression of its eyes, nose and mouth. Soon, where it had burned through completely, I could see the black void that was usually blocked from my view by the mass of demons. The body was draining into it, returning to the nothingness it had come from.

I ran into the storeroom and retrieved some of the ink for filling in holes. When I came back, the body was gone, though the hole in the shape of the demon's face was still there. I knew if I left it long enough the nothingness would start to seep through, transforming into more demons as it passed the demarcation of the vanishing ink.

I had already witnessed this evolution once before after my parents had safeguarded the store with the vanishing ink they had prepared for it. For weeks the bucket had sat in our kitchen as the nothingness moved closer and then became a self-evident presence when patches of it began to appear on the horizon. Many people in town tried to flee, but they came back to report that the nothingness had surrounded us. We had become a floating island just a few miles across and what space was left to us was shrinking every day. The despair was unbearable to me. I did not fear for myself – that fear I left to my parents – but to see the few people left around us, friends, neighbors, other shop owners, so crushed by the despair of the imminent destruction of every bit of life any of us had ever known, and knowing all the while that a solution that could save us all was sitting in a bucket in the kitchen, was unbearable to me.

"Do we have enough ink to save the town?" I asked my mom.

"We barely even have enough for the shop," she told me.

"How many people do you think we can fit in the shop?" I asked.

"Sweetie, this is not going to be easy to understand, but we're only going to use this ink for the three of us."

"What? Why?" I asked, but didn't give her a chance to answer before I went on, "what about my friends and their parents, what about uncle Mark and aunt Judy, what about –"

"We can't save all of them," she shouted, "we're going to be lucky if we can even manage to save ourselves."

That stopped me. In all the chaos that had surrounded us I hadn't even once doubted the certainty that they would see me through alive. I knew others were dying in other parts of the world, but I thought we would be spared; that nobody I knew would die. I think my mom realized what a weight she had dropped on me because she quickly added, "sweetie, your dad and I are going to do everything we can to get the three of us through this. Times like this require great sacrifice and hard decisions. We wish we could save everyone in the world…"

But I had stopped listening, burdened as I was in equal parts by this sudden understanding of the unstoppable destruction coming down on us and by how quickly my naivete towards it had been destroyed. I aged ten years in those few moments. When my mom stopped speaking I said, "yes, okay," not even sure if it was a coherent response, then went to my room.

For weeks afterwards, as friends came to say goodbye to us and as the life in our town descended from despair to chaos, all I could see when I looked at anyone else (including my reflection) was death. The fires that burned day and night, the noise of looters, the screams of women being raped and men begging for their lives all suited my mood to an alarming degree – what a state I had gotten myself into to be a twelve-year-old boy who took comfort in such a symphony.

My parents decided to take action and protect ourselves the first time anyone threw a rock through one of our windows. They said their plan had been to wait until the nothingness was closing in before using the vanishing ink, but the morning after the window-smashing they were outside our sidewalk with their largest quills, drawing a barrier on the ground. I thought it would make everything on the other side invisible to us but, as my dad explained, someone or something had to actually cross the line for it to work. I got my first demonstration of this when a bird almost flew into our store but vanished when it crossed the line. A few days later a few strays from a mob charging down the street tried to attack our shop. Their sudden disappearance stopped the rioters in their tracks and an eerie calm settled on the street such as we had not heard for days. I watched them from my bedroom window and saw among them so many of the faces of friends and relatives who I had wanted to save just a few days before.

I had been so isolated from the chaos of the streets that I had not realized just what kind of madness had come to grip them, but I could barely register the faces I saw out there as human. I remember thinking at the time (with no notion of the irony to come) that it was as though demons had stolen their faces and were wearing them as masks. There was no love or thought or intelligence in those eyes. There is in fact no word for what I saw except nothing.

For the first time in weeks I felt some sense of security again. The rioters left our shop alone and quickly our new state of affairs began to seem normal. My parents continued to mix ink with what supplies we still had in the shop, mostly inks for food and water. I had grown up watching them mix inks and so for awhile I gave no thought to their labors, but it started to bother me that they worked so studiously at it.

"What's the point?" I asked them one evening, "if the nothingness destroys everything except our shop, then why bother? We're just going to die anyway."

They winced at the question.

"Things aren't that hopeless, sweetie," my mom said.

"You think we haven't been planning for that, son?" my dad added, then gestured for me to come over. He had a notebook in front of him, the notebook he used to write out ink formulas. Though I hadn't quite learned how to read them yet, I understood something of their language. A formula for a simple ink, like for drawing water, required only a few words and symbols, but a more complex ink, like for brewing thunderstorms, required four or five lines to write out. I had never seen a formula longer than seven lines but the one he was working on took up the entire page, or so I thought, until he started flipping back through the notebook to show five, ten, twenty, thirty-four pages of formula.

"What kind of ink is that complicated?" I asked

"An ink like no one has ever even attempted before," he said, "it's an ink that will let us draw a new world. With one jar we can create an entire new earth from scratch. It'll be a great opportunity to build a perfect world, or at least a better one than this, one where there is no nothingness, where everything will be beautiful."

"But how will we populate it?"

"I don't know. We might have to take solace in filling it with plants and insects and leave the course of evolution to take over again, but maybe we'll be able to mix an ink that will let us draw people into existence."

"If the ink works," I said.

"Yes," my dad sighed, "if the ink works."

#

I don't know why that demon alone attempted to enter, but it has been a long time since any of them tried to get in here. Most of them can't get past the line my parents drew, but I've never understood why. I suspect that, even with their wicked smiles, they fear the something as much as I fear the nothing. It requires only the one though, who sneaks past unnoticed and comes to my bed as I sleep, to put an end to me and what little of the world I have left to myself.

I still had the ink, but when my parents died they took with them the secret of how to make them and how to tell them apart. So familiar were they with each of their inks that they never labeled the jars they came in, discerning instead from the thousands of inks by scent, pouring out the customer's requests by their nose. The smells have no logic to them. An ink with the scent of lemons produced a length of rope, but the smell of sulfur drew a bouquet of roses. Eventually, through trial and error, I catalogued what inks did what, and now I do what I can to manage my dwindling supplies.

But there is one ink in particular I search for, one among the thousands of inks that just may be my salvation. I remember the weeks my parents spent brewing it. I had never seen them put so much work into a batch of ink, mixing ingredients I'd never seen them use before. Eventually they produced a jar that looked no different from any other but whose scent was never the same no matter how many times I smelled it.

"This is the accomplishment of a lifetime son," my dad said, "an ink that can draw new worlds. No one's ever made it before, we're the first ones to ever do it."

And then they died before they could ever use it or remind me which among the thousands of jars it was. I'm alone now, with no hope except to find the ink, one among the thousands of jars under the watchful eyes of the demons.

A demon found its way into my room. I screamed when I awoke and saw it hunched over on top of my desk. It was a fraction of the size of the one I encountered the other day, tinier, in fact, than any other I had seen in glimpses out the window. It made no response to my cry, nor any reaction when I sprung forward with the knife I kept under my pillow for a purpose such as this. I stopped short just as I was about to bring the blade down on its neck. It was using my nature inks to draw a meadow on the desktop.

I set down my knife and put my hand into the meadow. It had been so long since I had felt wind that even the breath of it on my palm was enough to awaken so many buried childhood memories – times happier than any I had known in a long time. I had sworn to myself that I would never forget what it was like to lie down in the grass, but it seemed such joys had escaped me after all.

My hand made the demon aware of my presence for the first time and it looked up at me. I didn't fear its eyes as I did those of the others. It showed a gentleness I had never witnessed in them before. Was this perhaps not a demon at all but some other creature so alike in outward appearance as to be inevitably mistaken for one?

As I was lost in thought it wrapped a tiny hand around one of my fingers so suddenly that I scarcely had time to react. I yelped at the touch before realizing how humane it was, its skin rough and cold, as it had probably just come from outside. It looked at me, then drew its eyes towards the meadow.

"Perhaps you should devour it as you have all the rest of this world," I said and snatched my hand away from it.

I spent the next many hours on my bed staring at the creature, wanting to trust it but afraid that if my eyes strayed from it it would use that moment to pounce and put an end to me. But it never did any more or less than stare at its meadow and occasionally poke at it to flesh out the trees or float a couple of clouds above the scene. Finally I came over and ran my finger along one of the tiny blades of grass and found I could stretch it out much as if I were sketching. The demon was staring intently at my work. I pinched the blade with both hands and molded it, making it resemble a leaf. I tried turning it into a tree, but the material was stretching too thin for that kind of manipulation, so instead I curled the leaf up, then knocked it over and fashioned it into a log, with mold growing on the topside. When I finished, the demon reached out and caressed my design, showing the kind of fascination I would expect from an infant.

Then I had an idea.

Delicately I picked up the demon, cringing at its texture on my skin. I carried it downstairs, holding it in front of me like a shield. The demons were gathered as usual around the shop windows, pressing their faces against them, more faces than ever it seemed, watching with intent at this new spectacle that paraded before them. The demon in my hand had not proven as much of a protection against the violence of their glares as I had hoped, but this was not why I had brought it down with me. Rather I was taking the profound risk of taking it to the storeroom, because I had an idea of just which ink it might lead me to.

When the demon saw the buckets lined on their shelves, it leapt from my hand and crashed against them, scattering ink in every direction. I panicked as I watched it toss my food inks against the wall, droplets transforming into tiny globules of bread, vegetables and pies as they spilled out. I lunged for it as it sent a bucket flying into the opposite wall, which then exploded into a display of fireworks, singeing my hair and burning holes in my clothes. Another bucket burst into bouquets of flowers, an avalanche of rope fell and entangled me, I slipped on the contents of another bucket that had marbles spilling out from it. And, just when I was about to grab it, it latched onto a jar on a shelf just above my head. I reached up and took it down with the demon still clinging to it. Unlike the other inks, this one was a swirl of colors that never stopped moving. How many times had my hands passed by this jar without noticing it before? My anger at the demon was forgotten as I dipped a finger in and drew a circle on the wall. I filled it in, then scooped the circle out of the wall and molded it into a sphere. It took on the appearance of a tiny planet. I had another idea. I picked up the planet, then stepped out into the main room and hurled it against the glass. For once it was the demons feared me as it splattered against the glass. They cleared away from where it hit and I caught a rare glimpse of the emptiness behind them from which the demons materialized.

"Perhaps you're not such a bad fiend after all," I said, picking up the jar it still clung to and taking all of us back upstairs.

I don't think I fear the demons anymore. I slept better last night than I have since before the branches of the trees started calling for me against the windowpanes.

I took the bold inspiration this morning to tear open the curtains on my bedroom window. There was no sign of the demons who usually perched out there. I can't recall my bedroom view ever being fully exposed to the abyss before and there is something so horrifying, yet beautiful, about the sight of the expansive vacuum. I found it strangely inspiring to sit before it and experiment with the ink.

It was like no ink I had ever used before. My first thought was to draw a meadow with it, as the demon had, but each stroke of the pen had a way of taking on a life of its own so that my attempt to draw a blade of grass somehow resulted in a stick figure who danced about the desk before jumping to the floor and running through a crack in the wall. I would try instead to let my hand do as it wished but the results were too random to be of any use. The only consistency I noted was that the outcome of my pen was always organic, and in testing this I attempted to draw a car and wound up instead with a jackal who was lively enough to try to bite my finger.

All the while the demon watched my efforts intently, never blinking as its eyes followed the movements of my hand. Its unyielding gaze began to wear on me, so to temper my annoyance I took my pen and swiped it across its cheek. To my astonishment the ink lightened its skin tone from black to brown. The demon looked up at me. Its expression was unreadable. I swiped my pen across its right eye and it turned from solid white to a deep, human brown. I followed suite with the other eye but found the sight of its human gaze staring out from that demon body to be, in a way, even more disturbing than the glare of one of the demons outside.

"What are you?" I asked, but it only stared at me.

I dipped my pen in the ink again and swiped it across the black slash of its mouth, which turned it into full, red lips. They tried to speak, but must have lost the trick to it, because all they could do was flap open and closed without making any sound. I turned the black scar of its nose into a fuller, plumper form. A thing of beauty, I thought, there is something divine beneath this crust, something, if not human, then cloaked in the beauty of humanity. I found myself becoming aroused by it, though I had no idea if what I uncovered was male or female. The world was devoured before I had a chance to find out if I was gay or not, and so I found the strokes of my pen quickened by the imminence of this discovery.

Its form was too tiny – I had to broaden my strokes to stretch its body out. With a vast sweep of my wrist I gave it arms that could embrace me. Its body took the form of a woman, with full, dark breasts; her skin was so much darker than mine, and smoother. I had never seen a naked woman before and here she was taking shape before my eyes, her body doing more of the work than my pen, guiding my lines through her movements.

I couldn't tell her ethnicity, and it could very well have been that she didn't have one. "Are you a real woman?" I asked her. She shrugged. I was unsure what to make of this. "Do you understand what I'm saying?" I asked. She smiled at me. There were still bits and pieces of the blackened flesh of a demon clinging to her skin and I spun her around to try to fill in whatever spots my pen had missed. I had a notion that perhaps completing her would grant her the power of speech, but the words never came, nor did her hair, for nothing grew on her scalp. Yet she was beautiful – more beautiful than I ever could have imagined.

"Where do you come from?" I asked. She pointed out the window, at a spot in the void. "Do you mean just from out there?" I asked and swept my arm in an arc. She shook her head no and pointed at the same spot. "What's out there?" I asked, but she only smiled.

I approached the window without fear, I think, for the first time in my life. I focused my eyes on the spot she had indicated, but no matter how much I wanted to imagine a lone light in the brightness, I could see nothing there.

"Are there other places like this?" I asked without turning away from my study of the emptiness, "other spots that survived?" Then I jumped as I felt something touch my back, then realized it was her hand. Before I could turn to her she wrapped her arms around my waist and I could feel her standing on tiptoes to rest her chin on my shoulder. I was startled by the tranquility I felt from her embrace. It had been so long since I had felt any kind of human contact. I twisted around in her arms to face her. Her eyes sparkled.

"I want to know everything there is to know about you."

I held my pen up to her face. She took it and, stepping away from me, began to draw.

I watched as she transformed my room into a likeness of the meadow I had first seen her create. She had a mastery of the ink that I couldn't fathom: she could flick her wrist and raise a crop of grass and, with an identical flick, spring forth a sunflower. With a few more twists and flourishes she populated it with an ark of mice, birds, raccoons and whatever other creatures she felt inspired to bring forth. When she finished, she turned and stared at me, her chin thrust out just a touch.

"You haven't answered my question," I said, but she only thrust her chin out more. There was something enticing in her stance, not just that she was naked, but that she seemed to be teasing me. Perhaps it was because she was so newly formed that I did not expect such sass from her.

I took a step towards her and she drew a fence between us. As I stepped over it she flicked the pen and raised it several more feet off the ground. The shot to my groin sent me toppling. Through the gagging pain I heard a sound that stopped my breath. Laughter. Her laughter. I stood up as best as I could manage.

"I want to hear your voice," I said, "you must speak beautifully."

She turned and beckoned me to follow her down the stairs, all the while dashing out casual creations with the pen. A quick swipe and a waterfall ran down the wall. Another flick and fish jumped from the stream below it. She glanced behind occasionally to smile as I followed her down the stairs. With a flick of the pen she drew a miniature sun that lit up the room as I had not seen it lit since customers regularly came through the doors. It was more than just the brightness (brighter than anything I had seen in years) that was painful, the illumination brought back more happy memories than I cared for. Every lighted corner recalled joyous old days – the time I stood outside that window over there and pretended to be a ghost watching the comings and goings of the store, a fantasy ruined by my mother and father constantly waving to me and pointing me out to smiling customers; the first jar of ink I ever sold, to an old lady who tipped me a quarter for being such a fine salesman; my mother pausing from organizing the shelves to watch the sun set through the front door.

I thought she was heading to the storeroom, but she only turned to it long enough to draw a veil of ivy to cover the entrance. She moved with divine randomness, drawing as it pleased her and by no logic that I could discern. I found myself growing bored of her creations and focusing instead on her figure. I never thought I would get a chance to know the touch of a woman and now that one of such godly beauty stood before me, turning the store I had lived in my entire life into a biosphere, I could think only of how badly I wanted her. She seemed to sense my thoughts, because she turned to me and gave an inviting smile.

"Can you tell me what I'm thinking right now?" I asked her, but she merely smiled again and beckoned me to follow her.

I would have followed her past the line that divided the store from the nothingness outside, or so I thought, until I saw that was where she was actually heading.

She forced open the front door, which whined on its hinges from the many years it had remained shut. The coldness of the vacuum outside chilled me even from a distance, yet she seemed not the least bit bothered by it. An edge of the sidewalk still remained, stopping where my parents had drawn the vanishing line so many years before. Not a demon was in sight. She stepped up to the rim, placed the nib of the pen at the edge, and drew an arc about six feet high. I say she drew, but the pen left no record of its passage, yet she seemed satisfied with her work. I stood several feet away and when she saw that I had not approached, she came to me, grabbed me by the hand, and marched me to the barrier. Standing so close to the nothingness was more terrifying than the manifestations of the demons, but she showed no fear. Instead, she stepped through her invisible doorway, vanishing as she crossed the line.

There had been no hesitation in her step, she had crossed as casually as if she were going into the next room. I stood stunned and alone, unwilling to follow though it was clearly what she wanted me to do. I recalled the words of my father, saying if I ever crossed the line the abyss would swallow me, but there was no place she could have come from except from the other side of it. I could feel her eyes on me. She was beckoning me, and I came to understand as I hesitated that even if I crossed to my death there was nothing waiting for me in the shop or my room. I wanted to be free from my memories, free from the walls, free to create new worlds with the Eve I had helped shape into being and who now held the promise of a different kind of future, one that was composed of something rather than nothing.

I could sense her laughter. I stretched my hand across the barrier. There was a peculiar lack of sensation interrupted by a faint tingling of warmth. I could feel her presence, feel her taking my hand. She was the only thing I had any faith in. I stepped across.

Adam Breckenridge is an Overseas Traveling Faculty member for the University of Maryland Global Campus, and travels world teaching American military stationed overseas. He's currently based in South Korea. He has eighteen short story publications and his fiction has most recently appeared in Clockwork, Curses and Coal from World Weaver Press, Mystery Weekly and Horror Addicts

A World of Broken Things

Kai Delmas

A World of Broken Things

A book slipped from my grasp and fell with an echoing thud.

Shit!

I froze. Just listened to the eerie quiet of the desolate library.

Nothing. No moans, no movement.

Sighing with relief, I checked my scribbled notes before grabbing some books. Big sciency ones.

God knew I didn't know squat about what I was looking for, but dammit, one of them could be what I needed.

The books lay heavy in my backpack on my trek home but I was close to an old pawnshop I used to frequent before the world went to hell and wanted to take a little look-see.

I crawled through the smashed display window because of the damn chimes hanging above the door. I didn't want to be ringing any dinner bells, now did I?

A shattered porcelain ballerina lay among the destruction. I gathered all the pieces I could find and was satisfied. Ears pricked, I headed home.

Safe inside, I retrieved the broken ballerina and placed her on my workstation. Mended figurines watched as I fixed her up, gluing everything back where it belonged.

As I finished, I heard a moan from below. I went to the fridge and pulled out a rotting slab of beef, opened the cellar door and threw it down.

Sighing, trying to keep tears at bay, my eyes wandered from the figurine to the books on viruses and *Biology for Dummies*.

I had to start somewhere.

Maybe one day I would be able to fix you, too.

Kai Delmas loves creating worlds and magic systems and is a slush reader for Apex Magazine. He is a winner of the monthly Apex Microfiction Contest and his fiction can be found in Martian and is forthcoming in Tree and Stone and several Shacklebound anthologies. Find him on Twitter @KaiDelmas

Eight Bar Blues and You Ain't Goin' Home

Wayne Faust

Eight Bar Blues and You Ain't Goin' Home

I'd been working in Chicago for over twenty years, reviewing nearly every two-bit act that came down the pike. So that makes it all the more remarkable that on the night when I first saw Jake Wilson perform, he blew me away.

It was an icy cold night in February, a hawk wind blowing in off Lake Michigan, and needles of snow swirling in the air. I was heading for the Shady Gator, a new place on Rush Street, nestled in among the trendy dance clubs and holo-performance venues that are so popular these days. I cursed my luck in having to leave my hi-rise to check out a new act on a night like this, but it was live music, so I went. There aren't a lot of live acts out there these days, but I happen to like them. Call me old-fashioned.

As I walked into the Shady Gator, it turned out to be a lot more old-fashioned than even I would have preferred. There was no enviro program, no holographic wallscreens, just plaster walls with the brick underneath showing through in patches. Imitation cigarette smoke seeped down from tiny holes in the ceiling. Rows of thrift shop, folding chairs faced the stage. It looked like a room that had been thrown together at the last minute for a poker game. Knowing what they charge for rent on Rush Street these days, I didn't believe it for a second. But the room was warm, so I took off my coat and sat down. I counted twenty people in the audience in a space that held a couple hundred.

Jake Wilson was already into his act. The stage was tiny, barely big enough to accommodate him, and looked like it was made out of plywood. He was sitting on a stool and playing a hollow-body Martin guitar, tapping his boot in time with the music. He worked a metal slide up and down the frets, making it sound like grown men crying. He was singing through a microphone that looked like it could have been around a hundred years ago, back in the early days of radio.

Sweat dripped down Jake's black-as-pitch face, sending little beads into the air as he swayed his head back and forth. A cigarette that almost looked like the real thing hung down from one corner of his mouth. A single blue light hung from a cord above his head.

He was playing the eight bar blues. I've always loved the blues, and in spite of the obvious gimmickry of the place, Jake's music was the real deal.

> *You got me runnin'*
> *You got me hidin'*
> *You got me run hide run hide any way you want*
> *Yeah yeah yeah*

What was it about that music? There was a slow, easy groove to it that took me to another place. Instead of February in Chicago, it was suddenly a summer night on the Mississippi delta with the air dripping; I was sipping lemonade and Jack Daniel's on somebody's front porch with my feet up, listening to a freight train dwindle in the distance. I felt like I had hitched a ride on a time machine, something only a very privileged few have ever done.

A deep sadness nibbled away at the edge of my consciousness. It's not okay to be sad these days. What's there to be sad about? Nobody's hungry. Everybody's got a nice place to live. We've got a billion kinds of entertainment at our fingertips. And pills for every possible situation. But still…

Some of the old recordings I've got at home make me feel a little bit like that, at three in the morning with the music coming out of the wall. Like most music critics, I'm a better listener than a player. But back in the day, given the right combination of pills, I would drag my old Gibson out of the closet and play a little myself - until my neighbor once pushed a handwritten note beneath my door. All it said was, "Please stop singing." I never did it again.

So I write. Tribune Universal is the fifth largest communication market in the world. I get wined and dined. People respect me. I'm supposed to be an impassionate observer. But here I was, riveted to my chair by Jake Wilson.

> *I laid down last night*
> *Tried to take my rest*
> *My mind got to ramblin'*
> *Like wild geese from the west*

For a panicky moment, I felt something well up inside and I thought I was going to cry. How would I explain *that*? But then I settled down, and the music soothed me like my Mama used to do.

At the end of the show, Jake stood up and took a hesitant bow. I clapped as long and hard as I could, hoping to coax an encore out of him, but the house lights came on. The crowd filed up the stairs. No one thought to stay around and shake Jake's hand or get an autograph. People are jaded these days.

But I waited. I sat alone in my chair and tried to hang onto the feeling the music had given me. A soft hiss came from the ceiling as vacuums sucked up the ersatz smoke.

Jake Wilson left the stage and brushed by me, looking straight ahead. He smelled like sweat and something else, a dusky, clinging odor that could have been what real cigarettes had smelled like in the old days.

I ambled over to Jake, who leaned on the bar with his hand wrapped around an antique bottle of Schlitz beer. They had thought of everything.

I cleared my throat. "Excuse me," I said. "I was wondering if I could talk to you for a moment."

"Ain't got no moment," he answered, looking away. His speaking voice was as raspy as his singing voice had been.

I touched the man's sweaty arm, more to reassure myself that he wasn't a hologram than for any other reason. His skin felt hot and slick. "Please," I said, "I just want to ask you a few questions."

Jake turned towards me. His eyes were bloodshot and there were traces of yellow on his teeth.

"Ain't nobody say please much around here," he said.

"Well, I would just like to talk with you a few minutes. I've never heard anything quite like I heard tonight, at least not live anyway."

"Oh, so you a fan," he said. "Barman will get you a picture."

"I don't want a picture - I mean, a picture would be fine, but what I really want is to ask a couple questions."

His eyes darted. "You a cop?"

"Of course not. I'm a music critic. But right now I'm not thinking about that."

Jake looked up at the ceiling. "Go ahead," he said.

"How do you do that? Nobody sings the blues like that anymore. Nobody *has* the blues. Why should they?"

"That what you think? Nobody got the blues here? They got 'em all right. It be in their eyes. They got empty spots, way inside. The music reach in there and fill 'em up. Better than any o' them pills."

The man was right about that. I'd felt it myself. "And what about you?" I asked. "What does it do for you?"

Jake Wilson took a long, slow sip of beer. "I just play," he mumbled. "That's all."

Someone tapped my shoulder. I turned to see a skinny little man glaring at me. His silver hair was flawless and he wore a suit that must have cost a few thousand credits. His tie had blue music notes on a black background and it was held in place by a diamond pin. I recognized him. To say that Tommy Buechler. had his fingers in a lot of different pies would be a real understatement. In the already shaky world of Chicago politics, this man was an octopus. I'd never met him, but I'd seen his picture a bunch of times. He'd always been a little on the chunky side but in person he looked gaunt, and the gray skin on his face sagged.

"Come on, Pal," he said. "We're closing up now."

"Can I have another minute? I'm Henry Atwater from the Trib. I'm doing a story on Jake Wilson."

Buechler's face brightened." You with the press? That's different." He stuck out a hand. "Tommy Buechler. I own this dive."

I shook his hand and wondered why a guy like Buechler would want to own a place like this.

"Ain't that the best, damn blues you ever heard?" asked Buechler.

I couldn't argue with him there.

"That's why I brought him here," said Buechler. "I opened this place just for him. I'll send you the official bio. What's the number?"

"I was kind of hoping I could talk to Jake for a few more minutes."

"Impossible," he said, frowning. "Mr. Wilson has a previous appointment. Isn't that right, Jake?" He glanced sideways at Jake, who set down his beer, stood up, and strolled through a side door into his dressing room. Just like that.

I gathered my wits and turned back to Buechler. "So, business been pretty good, Mr. Buechler?" I asked.

"Call me Tommy," he said. "Everybody calls me Tommy." He flashed a weak smile, and his blue eyes sparkled for a moment. "You know how it is. It takes a while to build up a following. Write us a nice article. That will help."

I gave Tommy my number at the Trib and headed towards the door. I glanced back over my shoulder and saw Tommy walk through the same door Jake Wilson had gone through and close it behind him.

Later that evening I sat at my kitchen table, nibbling on kiwi fruit and rice. I popped a white pill and washed it down with pomegranate juice. I needed peak serotonin levels if I was going to write Jake Wilson the review he deserved. He should have been playing the Jordan Center, and if I had anything to say about it, he would.

I clicked on the wall screen and the rain forest filled up the room. I logged on and dictated my review, starting over several times until I had it just right. I sat back, satisfied. I had given it my best shot. Maybe it would bring in a crowd for Jake.

My brain was still racing from the pill, so I logged onto the Trib's database. Jake's bio said that he had been born in Amelia, Louisiana, so I ran a search of the birth records for the past 50 years. No Jake Wilson. Nothing in Terrabonne Parrish either.

He could have been using a stage name of course, or the whole bio could have been phony but I didn't think so. He seemed like the real thing, and besides, if you were going to come up with a stage name, you would probably come up with something a little more flashy than 'Jake Wilson.'

I planned to ask Buechler for a few more details the next night when I went back to see Jake. For the first time in my life, I had become a fan. I swallowed a black pill and headed off to bed as the rain forest winked off behind me.

The next night I had to stand in line at the club, even though light snow was falling. I squeezed through the door and grabbed one of the last available chairs, way back in the corner. Jake came out on stage and parked himself on his stool. He didn't say hello to the audience, didn't smile, nothing. He just started singing. Thankfully, the music was as good as I remembered from the night before, maybe even better.

I glanced back and saw Tommy Buechler leaning against the bar. He gave me a thumbs up. A waitress brought me a beer and said it was from Tommy.

After the show I waited for Jake to come to the bar, but he disappeared into his dressing room. As I stood to leave, Tommy came over and thanked me for the rave review.

"You're welcome here any time," he said.

"Don't mention it," I said. "The man deserves it."

"Yeah," said Tommy. "He's an original, all right."

There was something about Tommy's manner that made me nervous. His eyes kept darting back and forth like he was afraid that he would get busted any minute. I supposed that was normal when you lived a life like his.

I climbed the stairs and stood outside in the snow, my teeth chattering. The rest of the crowd had filtered away and I was alone on the sidewalk. A few cars purred by overhead, the whine of their engines muffled by the cold. The sounds of dance music wafted towards me from down the block but at this distance it was just a rumble of thumping bass notes.

I scanned the building. Was there a back door to this place? Would Jake come out that way? I put my hands in my pockets and strolled into the gangway. An alley cat hissed at me from a trashcan.

There was a door in the side of the building. I paced back and forth in front of it, feeling like a kid waiting outside Soldier Field for his favorite player to come out of the locker room.

The door opened and Jake Wilson stepped through, head down. He bumped into me and looked up. "You again," he said. "What you want?"

"I'm sorry if I startled you. Can I buy you a beer or something?"

"What for?"

"No special reason. I thought maybe we could talk. I wrote that review and..."

"That why all those people were there tonight? You write somethin' good?"

"Well, yeah."

"Thanks. That real nice but the man don't want me talkin' to nobody."

"Look, it won't take long. I know a place just down the block. The beer's real cold."

Jake looked back behind him, towards the door.

"Come on," I said. "Just for a few minutes. There's so much I'd like to ask you."

"I be a little thirsty," he answered. "Besides, I ain't nobody's *slave*."

The word slapped me in the face. Once upon a time somebody might have called *me* that but now it was just a word in the history books.

"Ummmm...okay, great," I said. "Let's go."

Michigan Avenue was busier than usual for a snowy night and it took us a while to find a place that wasn't jammed. We settled on Duffy's, my favorite little Irish place, and one of the few pubs in Chicago that hasn't yet given in to the virtual slots business, with its rows of flashing lights and the annoying sound of credit chips piling up in stainless steel trays. There's nothing but a mahogany bar, some comfortable booths, and Guinness on tap.

We took a booth in the corner and I ordered us a round. Evidently Jake had never had Guinness, because he coughed when he took his first sip and mumbled something about it tasting like tar. But he drank it down fast and we started on seconds.

"Where did you learn to play like that?" I asked. "From the old recordings?"

"Ain't had no recordings."

"Then who taught you? What program?"

"Ain't had no program."

"Then how did you learn?"

"I just do it, that's all. I sing from here." He pointed to his heart.

I couldn't argue with that.

We drank in silence as I tried to think of something else to ask.

"I wanna ax you something," he said.

I looked up. Jake had never initiated conversation before. He was starting to slur his words and I strained to understand his thick, bayou accent.

"Time," he said. "What you know about it?"

"What do you mean?"

"Travelin' in time. Goin' back. Or frontwards."

"Well, you know. Everyone knows. They have a few portals but the government keeps a really tight lid on them."

"Could they go back and kill somebody?"

I set down my beer. Why was he asking me this? "I guess somebody could," I answered, "but it's real illegal. If you killed somebody in the past you might screw up the present. That's why it's so controlled. But yeah, I suppose you could go back and bump somebody off. Theoretically. Why?"

Jake's hand gripped his glass until his knuckles turned white. "I gotta go," he said, and he stood up unsteadily.

"What? Wait, I'll take you in my car..."

But he was already gone.

Later that night I hit the databases again. My thinking was still a little fuzzy from the Guinness so I popped a purple hangover pill. Something smelled really bad here. I had called Louisiana that morning and no one I talked to had heard of a blues singer named Jake Wilson. I read as much as I could about Tommy Buechler. It seemed that he had connections in more places than just Chicago - my wallscreen lit up with six foot high pictures of Tommy with all kinds of famous people - entertainers, movie stars, rock stars, even the Prime Minister of Japan. I wondered how I hadn't run across Buechler before, because I'd met a lot of those people myself - except the Prime Minister of Japan, of course.

I shut off the screen and sat back. The pieces of the puzzle were coming together. I didn't like the picture they were starting to show.

The next night I showed up early at the Shady Gator and grabbed a seat up front. When Jake came out on stage he seemed afraid to look in my direction. It didn't affect his music, though. It was great as always, especially from the front row, and I found myself drifting back into that zone. Jake sang and the lyrics flowed out of him like smooth whiskey.

> *It's the last fair deal goin' down*
> *This the last fair deal goin' down, good lord*
> *On this Gulfport Island Road*
> *I'm workin' my way back home*

He eased into the solo, bending the B-string and coaxing a soft whimper out of the note, followed by a hammered G in the bass line. It was a beautiful touch that connected to something in my brain. Where had I heard that lick before, on that song?

I have an old recording at home. It's exceedingly rare, at least a hundred years old. It's *Last Fair Deal Gone Down* by Robert Johnson, still on vinyl, still in the original packaging. I never shared it with anyone, never transferred it over to data, nothing. It must be worth a lot of credits, but I've always kept it to myself. The recording has the same lick that Jake had just played.

Where had Jake learned it? From the same recording? That seemed impossible. There was only one explanation.

For once I wished the show were over. It was time to have a talk with Tommy Buechler.

Jake finished his last song and headed straight to his dressing room. I walked over to the bar as the crowd filed up the stairs. Tommy came out of the back room. I motioned him over.

"You're getting to be quite a fan," he said with his usual weak smile.

"You took him, didn't you?" I said.

"What?"

"Jake. You nabbed him."

Tommy's eyes flashed and the air turned to ice. I wasn't used to dealing with guys like this but I blundered forward.

"You know what I'm talking about," I said, spitting the words. "You got yourself a ride in a portal and you nabbed him."

Tommy's hands clenched and I thought he was going to haul off and punch me. Then, without looking away, he gave a quick, ominous flick of his wrist and the bartender went into the back room.

"What are you, a cop?" Tommy asked, holding me with his gaze.

"No."

"Then what's it to you?"

"He doesn't belong here. Can't you see that?"

Tommy snapped his fingers. "I could have you killed. *Just like that*." I should have foreseen this.

"Fine," I said, improvising. "Then the Trib will run my story."

"What story?"

"The one that will file automatically if I don't come home tonight."

Tommy hissed through his teeth. "I've got friends."

I didn't let up. "If there's even a *hint* that you broke the Time Laws, they'll be here in a heartbeat. Even you can't get away with something like that."

Tommy stared into my eyes for a long moment. Finally he turned away. His gaunt body seemed to deflate, and he suddenly looked very tired. "What did I get myself into?" he mumbled, looking down at the floor. There was a long pause as he gathered his wits. Then he stood up straight again.

"Okay," he said. "You wrote us a great review. I owe you one. So I'll give you some information. Off the record. And no cops."

I was amazed that he had given in so easily. He clearly wasn't the intimidating presence he might once have been. Now he looked like a tired, sick old man.

"We'll see," I answered.

Tommy cursed under his breath and then held one hand in the air, palm out. "God's honest truth," he said. "I nabbed him, just like you said. He was playing the Sweet Lips Lounge, Belmont and Halsted, August 25th, 1957. Can you believe that? It was over a hundred years ago. And I was *there*. We just wandered into the place. But I did know something about it. There was gonna be a fire in the club that night. Everyone was gonna die, including Jake. Charred beyond recognition. For once in my life I thought I had a chance to do something good for somebody before I kicked the..."

Tommy broke off and gazed at the stage. "You've heard him play," he said softly. "Wouldn't you have done the same thing?"

"But it's against the law," I said. "And for a very good reason. How'd you get on the portal?"

"Now that's something you don't need to know."

"Why Jake Wilson? Why not Beethoven or John Lennon or somebody like that?"

Tommy shrugged. "I didn't plan this ahead of time. We were there to witness the fire, a nice clean break, so we wouldn't change anything. But I didn't expect the music to be so…amazing. He never even did any recordings. It would have been lost forever."

"What if I spill the story?" I asked.

"You go ahead," Tommy said. "File your story. Then they'll come and get me. But they'll also come and get Jake. And they'll send him back. It's the law. And then he'll die. You might as well go stick a gun to the man's head right now and pull the trigger."

I wanted to rekindle my anger, to put my hands around Tommy's scrawny neck. But he had me.

"Did you threaten to go back and kill Jake's family?"

Tommy's eyes darted. "I had to tell him that. Otherwise he would have taken off. Can you imagine him wandering around a city that's a hundred years ahead of his time?"

"I'm leaving now," I said.

Tommy stood up and I thought he was going to block my path. But he just stepped aside. He must have been pretty confident that I wouldn't tell anybody. As I walked down Rush Street towards my car, I wondered if he was right.

That night I took a whole handful of pills. I felt like an accessory to a crime but what was I supposed to do?

I tried the databases. No one had kept very good records of poor blacks in Louisiana in the early 1900's. I found a Jake Wilson, born in Amelia in 1914. That was probably him. There were a few sketchy details about his life, but nothing else. I shut off the screen.

As I watched Jake perform the next night my heart ached for him. He sat up there and sang his guts out about losing everything and now I knew it was all real. But I just couldn't bring myself to even think about getting him sent back.

After the show I again waited for Tommy.

"Well?" he said.

"Well what?"

"No cops have been breaking down my door. I guess you didn't run that story."

"Not yet."

"Oh."

"Her name is Sally," I said quietly.

"What?"

"Sally. That's Jake's wife. The one he thinks you're going to go back and kill. I don't suppose you're really going to do that, are you?"

"No, of course not," Tommy admitted. "You don't know how many favors I used up the first time."

"I want to talk to Jake," I said. "He needs to know the truth. That's the only way I don't spill the beans."

Tommy looked like a trapped rat. "Okay," he finally muttered. "Tomorrow night. Jake gets here about an hour before show time. You can talk to him then."

All that night I couldn't sleep. I thought about my job. Was this what I was really meant to do? I had been at the Trib for twenty years. If I had ever had any passion for the music I reviewed it was long gone. Jake's music had brought some of it back but there was only one Jake. It would take a lot of pills to keep me doing this for twenty more years. I drifted off to sleep eventually, very late.

I walked into Jake's dressing room the next evening. It was a half-hour before show time and he sat alone, tuning his guitar. He didn't shy away from me so I guessed that Tommy had given him the okay. I pulled up a chair.

"I know what happened to you," I said.

"You mean how they come get me?" he asked.

"Yeah. But I think you should know something. Tommy Buechler isn't going to go back and kill anyone. He can't do that."

"You sure?" Jake's rheumy eyes opened a little wider.

"Promise," I said.

"That good," he said, and he leaned back in his chair. "So when can I go home? This ain't much of a place to be."

I knew that this question had been coming. How could I answer it? I decided on the truth.

"They could send you back. As of matter of fact, if anyone finds out where you came from, they have to send you back."

"Well alright," he said, his eyes brightening. "Sally be waitin' for me."

I paused, feeling hollow in my gut.

"You need to understand something," I said. "When they came and got you, they saved you from something that was gonna happen later that night. There was a fire and the Sweet Lips burned to the ground. Nobody got out alive. If you go back, you'll die too."

Jake pursed his lips. Sweat was running down his forehead even though the room was chilly. "But if I go back and know what happens, why can't I just leave *before* it happens?"

I sighed. "It doesn't work that way. You'd have no memory of being here, no memory of what I just told you, and everything would happen the way it was supposed to."

Jake squinted his eyes and he suddenly looked a lot older. I could see the wheels turning as he tried to understand.

"So I go back and I'm…dead?"

I nodded.

"And Sally…"

"She'll still be a widow."

There was a long, long pause. All I heard was Jake's raspy breathing and the rumble of the crowd gathering in the other room. Finally, Jake looked into my eyes.

"I ain't never goin' home no more?" he asked, his voice breaking.

"No," I answered."

There was another awkward pause as Jake looked down at the floor and shook his head.

"So I just another sad *slave*, standin' on the shore, lookin' cross the ocean, knowin' he can't swim."

There was that word again.

"I can check on your wife," I said. "To see how things turned out for her."

Jake lifted his head. "That be good," he whispered.

"And kids. Did you have any kids?"

"No," he muttered. "We were gonna have some but I guess we run out of time."

Jake stood up as the sounds of impatient clapping came from the other side of the door.

"What will you do now?" I asked.

"Sing the blues," he said. "Should be easy now."

"Jake?"

"What?"

"Could you teach me a few things? I have an old guitar from my grandfather."

"Old guitars is best," he said.

The clapping got louder. Jake wiped at his eyes. "Be here tomorrow night, after the show," he said, as he stepped through the door and out onto the stage. Applause erupted as the door closed behind him.

I stood up and took a clear plastic case out of my pocket. I opened the lid and grabbed a handful of colored pills. Clearly, I needed help and this should do it.

I stood there a moment staring at the bright colors in my hand. What would happen if I didn't take any pills? Would my head explode? Like everyone else, I'd relied on them for so long that it was hard to imagine a world without them. A world like the one that Jake had come from.

I knew it was crazy, and I knew I'd probably regret it. But at the last moment, instead of popping the pills into my mouth I tossed them into the toilet. Then I tipped up the case so the rest of the pills fell into the bowl as well.

The pills melted into the water in tendrils of bright, Easter egg colors. They swirled together until the water was a drab, dirty brown color. There was no bright orange, no purples, no reds. And no blues.

It was then that I knew what Jake Wilson had done. He had brought back some of the colors.

I flushed the toilet and the noise mingled with the sounds of the eight bar delta blues, coming through the dressing room door.

<hr>

Wayne Faust, *from Colorado, has had over 50 stories published in various places around the world. He's also been a full-time music and comedy performer for over 45 years, playing in 40 US States, and in England, Scotland, Holland, and Mexico. (www.waynefaust.com). From writing songs all those years, where you have to say everything you need to say in three verses or less, his prose tends to be tightly-written and fast-moving.*

The Cauldron of Metamorphose

James Rowland

The Cauldron of Metamorphose

Eilidh sat with her puffins on the cliff and painted with the sea. Her legs dangled over the side, some fifty feet above the waves crashing against the rocks. She moved her hand through the wind. Reaching out, she shifted the sands beneath the sea. The waves split off in new directions and shapes. Her eyes turned up and the sky became dark and hazy, clouds as brushstrokes, creating the contrast for the vista she could see in her mind. What was left was a masterpiece, a chaotic swirling of blues and whites, dancing under the darkened skies. She admired it for a moment. She let the view sink into her memories. Then the magic fell away and nature reasserted itself, a servant no more. Eilidh smiled at the puffins around her, the birds looking up with their orange beaks, quizzical, silently wishing she would hurl fish from the sea. Laughing, Eilidh shook her head and stood up. Not even her greatest spells, even the ones that gave the birds voices, or transformed them into all manner of companions, could distract them from their one true longing: food.

She left the puffins there perched on the cliff, waiting for their dinner, as she walked back to her hut. Atop the island, she heard the music first this time. Picking out the faint crashing symphony folded into the wind, Eilidh's body stiffened. She clenched her fists. The waves came crashing over her a moment later. Her breath froze in her throat. Her hair rose on end. Eilidh wrapped her arms tight around herself and tried to remember what warmth felt like. Another moment, her lungs burning, gasping for air, and the wave was gone. Eilidh stood alone on the hill on the island, on her island. She patted herself down, checking for any sign of the waves' embrace, wet fabric against her skin. She was dry. Like she always was after one of these strange attacks. Instinct demanded she check all the same.

Eilidh didn't understand the waves. Even now, she looked around the island. She stood on Staffa; a glorified rock hurled into the sea. It was true that the waves crashed against the shore and into the Cave below, but Eilidh wasn't there. She lived on the grassy surface that might as well have been the hair of some giant's head. The waves couldn't reach this high. Perhaps, it was just a part of her exile. A curse they had placed on her as they left her on the island and rowed away, condemning her banishment.

Taking a deep breath, her muscles relaxing, Eilidh continued her walk back to the hut nestled in the small valley on Staffa. It was sheltered from the wind, giving her a little comfort even in the bleakest winters. As modest as an honest monk, she had grown the hut from the weeds themselves. She reached out to the earth, wrapping herself around the strands. They grew. They fattened. The grassland shifted and took form, walls appearing from the ground. There was nothing inside it except a raised patch of soft vegetation, a bed for her to rest on. A cat sat on it. It was tiny, barely much more than a kitten, and its black fur was interrupted with patches of white and a dot of bright orange upon its nose. Eilidh wasn't sure how long her spell would maintain this form, but she was sure that all witches, banished or otherwise, needed a cat.

"How are my sisters?" the cat said.

Lowering her head, Eilidh walked inside and sat down on the bed. She sighed. "Hungry. Like usual. They didn't care about my painting."

"And did you bring back any fish?"

Eilidh rolled her eyes. "They said they would save you some."

"Perfect," the cat purred, sliding off the bed and out of the door in almost a single, graceful movement. Eilidh shook her head. You could remake the puffin into something else, but you couldn't change its heart's true desire. Maybe that was why she had never twisted their form into that of a human, to grow out its limbs and change its face until she had something more to keep her company than fish-obsessed birds and strange wave attacks. She wasn't sure she could take rejection in favour for the search of more trout.

Swinging her legs onto the bed, Eilidh laid back and stared up at the ceiling, weeds knotted together. When it was wet and cold, it was a grateful sight. Today, though, it felt like a prison. She hated it. She lifted a hand and flicked her wrist. The ceiling untied. Strands of grass slipped free of each other, suddenly eels, dancing away as the top of the hut opened up. The lingering, pale orange of the sunset hung above her and already the moon was taking its seat upon the pedestal of night. Eilidh smiled and sank into her bed of soft earth, watching as the colour drained away into darkness.

There were worse forms of punishments. Eilidh knew other girls in other villages hadn't been granted the gratitude and mercy of a banished life. When she was just a babe in her mother's arms, a witch had been pulled from her cottage, tied to the stake and then burnt for three days as the wind shrank from its task. Another had been tied with ball and chain while the men cut through the ice. They dropped her through the hole. The lake never unfroze. These women were snuffed from life. Eilidh relaxed in banishment. With her animals, she ruled her island. She was Circe reborn, a witch who made her prison her stately manor. She painted with the seas, she slept with skies, she walked across her windswept home and she played with her animal companions. It was hardly a punishment at all.

Men came sometimes too. They heard of the beautiful witch who ruled Staffa. Some men came with sails and Eilidh would watch them from her cliffs, slapped around by the winds. If she was feeling generous, she'd shift the currents just enough to give them safe passage back to the mainland. Often, she just watched them until the night swallowed the struggling figure. Those who rowed, though, would land on the beach. They'd take hold of their boat with strong hands and heave it up the sand. They knew better than to leave it bobbing in the sea. A boat will abandon its master with enough encouragement from the waves. Most of these men were ruffians, ready to pluck her from her home. Eilidh waited for them. They walked to her hut and she plucked them from the island. The winds came and wrapped its hand around their tiny bodies. They flew so far.

Occasionally, when the breeze was just right and the clouds vanished to leave the sun unmolested in the sky, real men came. They sat with her and talked. They hadn't meant to come to Staffa but were blown off-course. They found they liked the witch who ruled there. With red hair and skin so pale that it bordered on snow, they sat and shared stories with her. All of them were concerned she was malnourished, her arms and legs more like the branches of a tree, but she smiled and said she was well here. She enjoyed their company too, took them to her hut, and then left them to stare glass-eyed at the horizon as they sailed away the next day alone.

"What did you do?" one of these strangers said one day, sitting with her on the octagonal columns that led down to the sea crashing against the black basalt. His name was Douglass and he smelt like morning. "Why did they send you here?"

Eilidh laughed but it had no energy to make it further than her lips. She wanted to pretend that she didn't remember, that it had been so long ago and it was a trifling little thing, long forgotten in favour of her new life. She didn't care about her family retreating deeper into the shadows of memories. It didn't plague her that her mother's face was blurred, details swallowed by time. It wasn't true, though. She knew her crime and the punishment still stung. "I cured people. There was a plague, a disease of some sort, and people were dying in my village. I went out to each house. I did so at night to try and hide it. I knelt by each bed and I dragged the sickness from their bodies. I saved everyone I went to. Not a single person died. Not a single person saw me except those I cured."

The implication waited in the air for Douglass to grab it. "Someone you saved betrayed you?" Eilidh nodded. He shook his head. "But surely you should have been picked up and thrown onto people's shoulders, paraded through the village like a hero?"

She laughed again, this time with vigour. "You fishing boys are all the same. You know nothing of the world beyond your boats. The plague was God's will. More importantly, it was the will of the men that the plague was the work of God. They had deemed prayer sufficient. I offended God and I offended the men by going against them. I couldn't be allowed to stay. They took me from my home, they carried me down to the shore and loaded me into the nearest boat like a bag of grain. No arguments. No attempt at compromise. They left me here on this island before the sun had even finished brushing against the top of the sky. But it's fine. I like it here. It's peaceful. Quiet."

"I can take you with me. No one will know that you escaped your banishment. My family lives alone by the sea, we barely see another soul except to trade what we can't make ourselves. You'll be happy. It's peaceful there too."

Sitting with the boy, barely a man, his skin freckled and his hair buckling under the force of the wind, Eilidh wanted to say yes. It sounded like a nice life, a pleasant one. She opened her mouth and found only one word escaping: no. The next day Douglass was gone. The next month, she wondered, with tears stinging her eyes, why she had rejected him. The next year, she barely remembered Douglass sitting on the basalt columns with her. It all fell away into the sea eventually.

Stars vanished, blinked out of existence as the inside of her eyelids replaced the sky. She could feel herself drifting away, sleep her only true companion. The waves came again. Even here, on the top of the island, in her little hut nestled in the bosom of the valley, the water came. It roared over her. Like a vagabond waiting outside the tavern for some coins to fleece, it roughed her up. Something punched her in the rib, like a boulder thrown up from the shore. The water rushed to fill her nose. A waterfall claimed her throat, pooling in her lungs. She coughed. Her body struggled to bring up the water. She rolled over, a thunderstorm in her ears, and she choked, nothing coming from her burning throat. She was going to die. And then, as fast as they came, the waves were gone. She was left on her bed of earth, as dry as a distant desert.

Eilidh slumped, her face pressed against the grass. She breathed in deeply. A voice in her head whimpered that the attacks were getting worse. She needed to find a way to stop them. The voice slipped away, becoming first an echo and then a memory as sleep came. It wrapped her in darkness and deposited her on the basalt columns that led to the Cave. She knew it was a dream. A storm had brewed overnight and the rain and wind whipped around her and she felt nothing, only the absence of cold. She knew it was a dream because instead of turning around and fleeing back to the haven of the top of her island, she walked along the blackened columns and toward the Cave. A glow, warm, golden and flickering, seemed to fill it. It was waiting for her.

Even on the mainland, as a child listening to tall tales by the fireplace, Eilidh knew what had lived in that Cave. A monster lived there. As tall as three men and stronger than a dozen oxen, the giant Benandonner had ruled this island from the Cave. The basalt columns that Eilidh walked down were the ruins of the causeway that he himself had destroyed in his fight with a rival far across the sea. She knew that if there ever had been a giant, it would be long dead. Her head told her, in calm, reasoned tones, that giants weren't real and even if they were, the great Benandonner couldn't possibly live in such a small cave. There was nothing to fear there. Eilidh hadn't ventured down to the Cave anyway. Not yet. Not until tonight, safe in the knowledge that she was lighter than a feather, the collection of thoughts stitched together to make up a dream. She was safe in her hut on the top of the island.

Continuing along the columns, her feet moving from one to the next, her eyes wandered from the Cave to the Atlantic. It waited right next to her, nothing standing between her and the churning, black sea. The waves smashed against the side of the island. It reached out for her body. She remained just out of grasp. Sure-footed, the basalt smooth against her skin, she moved through the mouth of the Cave, its great top lip hovering above her. Her breath caught in her throat. A shiver started in her neck and danced down her spine. The Cave was illuminated by a sea of candles, floating through the air, suspended from the strands of her dream. Under their orange glow, Eilidh saw the basalt columns continuing, a staircase into the heart of the Cave. Beneath her, the water churned and crashed against the rocks, the floor of Benandonner's home just an extension of the Atlantic. There was no relief here.

Closing her eyes, the orange haze still seeping through, Eilidh breathed in and readied herself to wake up. This was enough exploring for today. Before she could end the dream, though, her heart stumbled off rhythm. She braced herself against the wall. Every muscle in her body went taut. She had heard it, the symphony of the waves crashing over to drown her, another attack reaching her even in sleep. She waited. She stood frozen on her little ledge. Seconds passed. The attack never came. Opening her eyes, Eilidh shuffled to the edge of the steps and glanced down into the churning water. The sound that stalked her across the island bubbled up from below.

The only thing Eilidh could hear in her little hut as she woke was the thundering of her own heart.

For a week, she tried to distract herself with other things. She marched down to the cliff and spun out voices for every puffin in reach. They croaked of fish and of fine breezes for flying. Conversation was beyond them. She took some of them and grew them into other pets, a menagerie of black, white and orange furs as cats, rabbits and dogs dominated the island. They would talk to her. They could even hold her attention for more than a few minutes at a time. It still wasn't enough to stop her thoughts turning back to the Cave. The attacks kept coming. She kicked out at the earth as another wave struck her from the top of the island. She screamed. It was endless. She marched from one end of Staffa to another in an afternoon, pausing to call the grass up. It stretched higher and higher, strands winding together, growing stronger, becoming fleshy, green lighthouses that dotted the landscape. She ran out of land all too soon. Banishment had finally snapped. Its teeth sank deep into her flesh. It left bitemarks in her sanity. There was only one thing she could do.

She waited until the clouds had parted. Descending into the Cave, where giants were said to live, and her curse seemed to draw power from, was already foreboding enough. She did not need the weather to provide further assistance. When the suffocating greyness did yield, though, Staffa looked beautiful in the midday sun. The island was bathed in light. Eilidh took her time to head down to the basalt columns and the Cave beyond. Sitting with the puffins, watching them battle the ever-present wind in their search for fish, her breathing steadied. She reached out to one bird and ran a finger along its back. It didn't move. It didn't take flight. When she stood up, though, her friends all took to the air and began to sing. They twisted and turned, flying in rhythm, a beat emerging as the flock took shape. A shimmering, curling spiral took to the air. It almost glinted in and out of sight. Eilidh couldn't escape the idea they were waving goodbye to her. She bit her lip and offered her own wave before walking away.

Eilidh's heart began its migration to her mouth as she walked to the Cave. In her dream, the weather was wet and wild, a villain lurching out from the shadows, but she knew the sea it worked with was toothless. She could not die. It was just a dream. Now, things were different. The waves still crashed against the edge of the island, rising up over the nearest columns. Eilidh walked higher up, pressed up tight against the cliff face. Each step was a knife, though. Each column frayed the edges of her nerves a little more. She wasn't sure how much further she could go before it snapped completely. All she could see was her foot slipping on the basalt, her body tumbling down toward the Atlantic, the waves snarling and striking out to grab her, her life disappearing into the sea. But she arrived at the mouth of the Cave without incident. Her island would not betray her.

The Cave was as beautiful in the day as it was in the dream-logic of night where it bathed in an orange haze. Eilidh continued to scramble across the columns, pushing deeper as the blueish green water churned and bubbled beneath her, crashing into the rocks. She looked down. For just a heartbeat, she thought of a witch and some cauldron. Maybe this was how she was being cursed. She frowned, swallowing back the urge to kick out at the column in front of her. It was nonsense. Witches didn't sit around in pointy hats, brewing potions over large, bubbling cauldrons. She knew that. It was just the shape stories needed to be to scare the right people. Somehow, somewhere, at some moment, the message had lodged deep inside the crevices of even her brain. The thought burned inside her. It gave her fuel to push further inside the darkening Cave.

The music of her attacks walked alongside her now, a constant companion. There was no doubt left inside her. The water crashing against the rocks was what Eilidh could hear just before she would be hit by the dry waves, pinning her down, forcing her to drown. She could hear her heart up in her ears now, a steady beating drum as she knew she was drawing closer to unravelling the mystery. The idea that there would be nothing awaiting her sat beyond the horizon of understanding. Eilidh could feel it in her bones. She was going to find her answers. A dozen images ran through her mind, cursed jewels and walls of herbs. She didn't expect to see the body.

Eilidh froze deep inside the Cave. She could smell the salt in the air, the spray stinging her eyes. In the darkness, she thought it might be her own shadow cast against the wall. Another step closer, though, revealed the chains. Her eyes followed them from the body, wrapped around the ankles and wrists, turning the figure into a star, and then snaked up the cave wall. The path ended with the chains looped around great metal rods, hammered into the rock itself. Eilidh tried to swallow, but even the muscles in her throat had turned to stone. She eyed the metal rods. She pictured men sailing into the Cave, climbing the columns, dealing with the wind and water, clinging to safety as they drove heavy iron bars into the very heart of the stone itself. It was a task worthy of song. Eilidh couldn't help but wonder what powerful evil must have led to those men taking such drastic action.

Rooted to the spot, she felt a tugging on her hands, both forward and back. Eilidh knew she could walk away. On the surface of Staffa, she could live with her puffins and her hut, and as Circe of the North, she could grow old in the playground of her own power. The attacks would continue to come, though. The waves would continue to swallow her. She needed answers. Eilidh took a step forward and then another. Her hands shook and her legs descended into the consistency of porridge, barely able to support her weight. They wanted to crumple beneath her. They wanted to throw her into the water below rather than confront the ancient evil chained to the wall. Though her body tried to betray her, Eilidh's mind and soul was as one, pushing through the sticky, clenching fingers of fear.

The closer she came to the body, the more it fell out of shadows. It sat outside the shape that Eilidh had built for it, tall and strong. Instead, she saw something short and slight, the figure slumped with its chin on its chest. Its dirty, knotted, red hair covered whatever face might exist behind the curtain. Eilidh noticed, with a gasp, the suggestion of breasts under that chin. She had expected a demon or a giant, not a woman. The woman on the wall was so pale that she bordered on snow and limbs seemed not much more than the weakest, undernourished branches of a tree. At Eilidh's approach, the woman lifted her head. Her hair fell back from her face to reveal skin drawn too tight over bone; lines etched deep into the surface. Whatever colour that might have existed was drained completely. It was Eilidh's face.

She had just enough time to scream and then the waves came and washed her away from the basalt columns and into the sea.

Eilidh opened her eyes in stages. The salt-encrusted grime tried to keep them shut, yielding in tactical retreats until she was finally able to see the Cave in front of her. She looked out and saw the suggestion of an existence beyond it, a world that hid just out of reach. Every inch of her arms and legs burned. Her muscles screamed in protest, stretched to their limits. There was nothing she could do about that. Her head lolled to the side and looked at the great metal rods buried inside the rock, holding her chains in place. She tried to groan in pain or protest, she wasn't sure which, but her throat refused to engage. She couldn't even move her tongue. Pinned to the cave wall, looking down at her prison, she wondered if it was just numb or if she even had a tongue anymore. She couldn't check.

Despite the agony, the cold, the numbness, the burning and the sheer exhaustion stitched into every part of her body, Eilidh knew what had happened. She didn't need to let the realisation sink in. It was already in her heart. She hadn't been Circe. It had been an illusion, a way for the shattered pieces of her mind to cope with the truth. She had never been Circe. Why would men reward her actions with freedom? It was the last thing of all that a man would offer. Instead, she was Prometheus and this was her real punishment. There was no liberation here, only chains. There was no magic to experiment with, only the stranglehold of boredom and pain. There were no puffins as friends, only two Great Skua, dark birds waiting to see if their newest feast was yet prepared. Her movement meant it was not. They took flight, but they would be back soon. It couldn't be long now.

But the illusion had brought her time. She had survived longer than they were expecting, birds or men. The chains felt weaker, screaming as she struggled against them. Just as Prometheus, she could not be chained here forever. She would escape. Eilidh braced herself as the tide surged forward. She heard the melody of the Cave, and then the waves crashed over her chained body. She could outlast them.

———◈———

James Rowland is a New Zealand-based, British-born writer. His work has previously appeared at Aurealis, Compelling Science Fiction, and Prairie Fire. When he's not moonlighting as a writer of magical, strange or futuristic stories, he works as an intellectual property lawyer. Besides writing, his hobbies are reading, travel, photography, and the sport of kings, cricket. Find more of his work at his website www.jamesrowland.net/

Wolf Whistle

Cheryl Sonnier

Wolf Whistle

Granny hasn't left her cottage in the woods since lockdown began, and your mum says, 'She'll be hungry, love. Take her a bite to eat; you know what she likes.'

Half an hour later, you're skipping down the path into the forest with a basket of goodies over one arm, and your blood-red cloak flapping in a wind that's grown teeth. As though on cue, he steps out from the trees with a piercing whistle. You step to the side to widen the gap to at least two metres, and hurry past.

'Cheer up, love.' He grins. "It'll never happen.'

You'd like to say, "If you're talking to me, it already has, mate," but you don't. You keep your eyes fixed on the path that disappears between the trees and increase your pace, without a glance in his direction.

Rule number one: don't make eye contact.

He follows, of course, overtakes and steps in front of you, his lantern jaw thrust proudly out and one hand on his hip, drawing attention to the over-sized chopper hanging from his belt.

'You know, you're prettier when you smile, Red. You should smile more.'

You want to tell him that your smile is not his to demand but you know from past encounters with his kind that your best course of action is to pretend you don't hear him. You dart around him and continue on your way. He calls out and you have to wonder why he's still following, if you're as fat and ugly as his petulant shouts claim, but you stay quiet.

Rule number two: don't let them see you react.

When his insults turn to threats, you start to run. He crashes through the trees in pursuit.

Rule number three: don't let them catch you.

By the time you reach Granny's cottage, it's close to dark. The wolf lies in wait on the porch.

You lay the basket on the step and sit down to catch your breath.

'Mum said you'd be hungry.'

'Did you have any trouble getting here?' she asks, nosing through the basket.

'There was a woodcutter,' you say. 'He followed me.'

Granny growls low and raises her hackles as he steps out from the trees.

'Good girl,' she says. 'I'm sick of soup.'

Cheryl Sonnier *lives in Leeds with her husband and two cats. She has an MFA in Creative Writing from Manchester Metropolitan University and her short fiction has appeared in* Cosmic Roots and Eldritch Shores, Plasma Frequency, Dark Futures, QWF *and* Roadworks.

Skin Deep

Celine Low

Skin Deep

It was the ink, I was sure of it. No matter how carefully I stencilled my designs, they always turned out strange. Once my needles pierced the skin, the colours seemed to *sink*—not just into flesh, but into reality itself.

This sleeve I was finishing for Mod, for example. My stomach was a tangled knot of nerves, because Mod Balig was the new leader of the Werewerms, the largest gang in Bel Loréth next to the Crazy Crows. The Werewerms were small but they were growing fast, fattening their purses from the monthly fees they squeezed from the shops within their turf. Mod didn't get to where he was without breaking a few heads, and if I wasn't careful mine would be one of them.

I straightened, stretching my spine. Mod's bedroom wasn't the most conducive place for inking—the chair was uncomfortably hard—but he'd refused to come to Skin Deep. I had to bring all my stuff to his, just so he could have a girl massage his feet at the same time. The girl knelt beside me now, slender hands kneading his calves. Her scent wafted over: wood and amber, slightly floral. Masculine, with a trace of feminine.

I told myself to focus, angling my head to examine my work. Something felt off about it, like everything I'd inked since I'd opened Skin Deep. Usually everyone had an aura, the vibes emanating from mood, personal history and the cloud of possibilities shimmering around an individual. I did my designs based on my perception of this aura, and if I was right, the customer would like my ideas. But recently, I'd been feeling that as I worked, the weave of reality around a person was being *re-stitched*. So much so that I was questioning my sanity. Because by the time I was done with each piece I could no longer sense the initial aura—only the inked image, crystallised in flesh.

Mod had asked for a dragon. A classic, nothing special, but Mod wanted a new marking for the Werms to show a change of leadership. So I'd carved a dragon round his arm, obsidian wings unfolding like thunderclouds eclipsing the sun. At the edges of my vision the dragon's scales rippled, deepwater-black and green. The air felt heavy, bloated with strange magic.

Mod fidgeted. The dragon moved with his muscles, rising and coiling, ready to strike. "Hold still," I snapped. My hand wobbled. A drop of ink fell on his pants.

"Watch it, boy!" Mod snarled.

Mod looked near to losing his temper, but thankfully the door burst open and a little girl scampered in, followed by a harried-looking woman.

"Papa! Papa!" the girl cried. "Risha slapped me."

"It was just—I didn't hit hard, I swear—she refused to—"

Mod shot to his feet, his face reddening. "How *dare* you hit my daughter?" His palm shot out; the girl's caretaker shrieked as it connected with her cheek. "Do I pay you to hit my children, huh?"

I flinched with every echoing slap.

Beside me, Mod's masseuse dried her hands on a towel. "He has a temper," she whispered to me. "It will pass."

The little girl, who had been watching with an impish smirk, now bit her lip. "Papa," she said, hugging his leg, "Papa, she didn't mean it, she didn't hit me so hard, and I was naughty."

It was like watching the end of a storm. Mod softened, picking the girl up and kissing her forehead.

"Still," he growled, glaring at the sobbing babysitter. "You're fired."

He settled his daughter on his lap, and barked at me. "Well?"

I jumped, muttered an apology the-gods-know-what, and dipped my needles again into the yellow.

The crusty yellow of blistered skin. The poison-yellow of wild parsnip. The cruel yellow of a desert sun.

Mod's masseuse leaned in to peer at my finishing strokes, her grey eyes widening in fascination. "So life-like," she murmured. Her skin was a velvety taupe-brown, silver under the light. "It's as if … it's tearing out of his skin."

Amber for the dragon's iris, like glowing coal. Cadmium flaring over veins of burnt umber. These were the shades I saw in Mod, a consolidation of his volcanic anger, his patient greed, his rough-hewn hunger. There'd been more to him when he'd walked in, I was sure, but now I couldn't see him being anything else.

Beneath my hand, black pupils narrowed into slits.

The inks had been left behind by Shu, the lady who'd sold me my shophouse. After spending all my coin on drink and inns, I'd paid her with the only valuable thing I'd had left—the gold stylus my parents had given me for my fifteenth birthday, two years ago.

Good riddance. It was a fine blade with an ornate handle meant for runewriting, but the complicated grammar and logographs of runes had never given me anything but headaches.

My mother was the Imperial Healer and headmistress of the Amari Academy of Bel Loréth, and she had never let me forget that I was Amari, too.

More precisely, that I was born to be a terraformer, like her. Amari have natural predilections towards different states of matter, and terraformers supposedly share the very essence of Earth—solids—just as tideraisers partake of the liquid character of Water, and windriders of Air, the gaseous element of steam and fire.

On nights when I particularly missed home, I'd dream of my mother. She had loved me, once. I dreamed of the gardens in our manor, the air thick with jasmine. My mother's hair glowing wheat-gold, twining itself into twigs and vines. Her hands reaching for me, the veins in her arms twisting into green tendrils. And her voice, ancient as pine. *This is your heritage—the shaping of stone, metal, soil, flesh. A skilled terraformer understands the workings of the body, and heals by moulding the dust from which man is made. Learn, and continue our legacy.*

She lifted a hand and a rowan sapling sprung from the ground, unfurling into a tree. *Vision and gesture*, she said, *the principles on which Amari power is founded. Ours is a weak remnant of the divine creative force, a leftover from the time gods roamed the earth. Have you learned the runes I showed you?*

I shuffled my feet. *But Amari don't need runes*, I whined.

Vision and gesture might command matter in the moment, but runes, like written contracts, keep a spell binding even in their author's absence. Otherwise, matter reverts to its natural laws.

She took out a stylus from the folds of her robes, the blade so sharp I only hissed in pain a moment later. Blood welled on my palm, forming intricate lines arranged in neat word-squares. *For protection*, she said, *against scrapes and bruises*. The rune shimmered, sinking beneath my skin. She moved her hand over mine and the cuts faded, but for a long time I felt it there, the weighty sting of her love.

That afternoon after I left Mod's house, his masseuse came to Skin Deep.

"What will you give me?" she asked, smiling at me with her eyes — teardrop-shaped and grey-green, like rainclouds scudding a forest lake.

I considered her swan limbs, the softness of her gaze, the hardness of her jaw.

"Wisteria," I said. She flinched.

I frowned. I usually got it right the first time.

Her aura flickered around her. I sensed a certain fragility, but a doggedness, too. "A candle-flame?" I hazarded. "A symbol of evanescence and the everyday fight for light in darkness."

She tilted her head, considering. "And of vulnerability, the flame naked without its paper-lantern dress." Then a rakish grin flashed over her face like armour and she leaned over the counter, her movements languid, feline. "Wouldn't you like to see me naked," she drawled. Her eyes gleamed, suddenly more green than grey.

"Um. What about the Trickster? Pékuras the shapeshifter, who escaped hell in the form of a cat."

In Lorétheian myth, cats could travel between the mortal and spirit realms. I pointed to a small sketch I'd done of a boy turning into a black cat, leaping into a white light while ghostly hands reached for him from beneath. "Patron of merchants and travellers," I added, in case she was one.

"A trickster?" She arched an eyebrow. "I assure you I'm honest."

"I didn't mean—"

She smirked, enjoying my embarrassment.

"Why wisteria?" she asked.

"Ištara's flower. Bliss, tenderness, immortality." I imagined a wash of purple against the cool undertones of her skin.

"The Loréthian goddess of love."

I nodded, shrugged. "I don't know the Bharan gods, but if you have an image I could copy ..."

"I already have them."

She raised a sleeve to reveal smooth skin. I stared, puzzled. Then she slid a hand over her right forearm and colour bled in, beryl-bright blue-green feathers with iridescent eyes. "The Creator," she said. She lifted her other arm, where stark black lines crossed to form twin spears. "And the Destroyer. God of death, war, retribution."

"You're a terraformer," I breathed. That wasn't why I was amazed; I knew that terraformers' flesh-altering abilities made them excellent at disguise, though they couldn't completely shapeshift. Neither was it the intricacy of detail that astounded me, nor the impossible vividness of hue. What caught my breath was the *weight* of each image, as if reality bent around it, answered its call.

"A Namer, like you," she said. "You glimpse a fragment of a person's soul and you draw it out. The ink seeps into flesh, mingles with blood. The body transforms, and the mind with it."

"This is … a kind of Earth magic?"

She nodded. "But this power isn't just something you're born with. It's also the medium—some inks, like Shu's, help you *see* things better when you're working."

I stared down at my hands.

"Your use of power doesn't make you less of an artist," she said gently. "Your design must be true, an image that binds to body and mind. Runes act the same way, like chains you can pull to command matter, and through matter, reality itself—just as the form and habits of the body sculpt the mind. And, like any art, truth can only be conveyed through technique."

With what little terraforming skill I had, I'd shaped a needle-brush that could vibrate the pins more quickly than human hands could move. This allowed me use horizontal strokes for subtle shading and soft gradients—a technique I was proud of. The girl's peacock feathers, however, were rendered with such precision that skin morphed into brilliant plumage, and as my eyes moved over her arm, each wispy strand billowed hypnotizingly as if touched by an imaginary breeze.

She dropped her sleeve, suddenly self-conscious. "I've never been able to do it for others. Only on myself. And there are parts of me that I can't reach."

How could I resist? She came every few days, disrobing before me while the summer sun warmed us through the window.

"How did a rich boy like you end up here?" she asked, once the awkwardness between us had passed. "You talk like you're from Jewel."

Bel Loréth was a city made up of two lake-islands, known colloquially as Jewel and the Claw. Each faced the other like its mirror image. But while the Temple was Jewel's crowning glory, Hogshead, the pleasure district, was the Claw's. Shortly after my fifteenth birthday, I'd hopped on a barge to Hogshead and never looked back.

"Why else would a rich boy cross over? To join the degenerates at Hogshead, of course."

She cast me a cool glance. "Did you like tossing coin at the women?"

I paused, startled. "I was usually too drunk for women."

Her shoulders remained stiff. I cringed at the impression I was giving, but I held her gaze.

"I hate it," she muttered. The vehemence in her voice surprised me. "This whole filthy city."

"Burn it down, then," I said mildly. "What's stopping you?"

She blinked, then laughed. "The sunstone and stained glass won't burn—didn't you learn this in school? The buildings won't get so much as a scratch. You need to make better jokes, boy."

"I make first-rate jokes, girl."

She smiled. "So how'd you end up here, all sweet and sober?"

"I was walking off a hangover. Saw an old man at Craft Lane, his client wearing a full suit. The old man's art brought that body to life."

How could I describe how my eyes had burned, the strange elation I'd felt at the sight of those colours soaking the skin, the promise of what I could do to guide a soul into its identity?

I could not. But from the way she was looking at me, I had a feeling she understood.

So I said simply, "I volunteered to be his assistant."

She nodded, turning back to face the window.

Her eyes drifted far away, reflecting the cerulean lake beyond. "Do you miss home?"

I thought of Jewel's stately mansions and sparkling canals, where I'd spent my happy childhood. My mother's disappointment had only shown as I'd grown older. She became sarcastic and bitter. She made herself take cruel measures.

We had a maid whose six-year-old son we took in after the maid died. After I'd failed my healer examinations, my mother brought him before me. He lay drugged on the carpet, blood seeping from a slit in his wrist. "Heal him," my mother commanded. She stood watching, arms folded, anchoring me to the chair with her roots and vines.

It wasn't a deep gash. Any terraformer could've done it in a heartbeat, just by sight. I sobbed. The pool of red spread across the floor.

I couldn't look at the boy, so I kept my gaze on the window, at the hill on which the Temple of the Thousand Gods glittered, stabbing the sky with its salt-white sunstone towers, its dazzling stained-glass spires. I remembered the stories told about these structures, how all this glass was blown by the Amari of old. My forefathers. I looked down at my hands.

I groped for my magic, until my eyes teared and my fingers ached. I wrestled against my mother's chains. I thought of the wisteria in the Temple courtyard, a tree old as the hills, its vast canopy dripping with the same purple vines constricting my legs. *Bliss, tenderness, immortality*. I prayed.

In the morning my mother knelt before the boy, crimson staining her robes. She closed her eyes, head bowed. Then she scooped him up gently, and left without a word.

I hadn't even known his name.

Mod's girl gazed steadily at me, her eyes flint-grey, piercing.

I gave a little laugh. "Other than the hot baths and rose-scented towels? No, I don't miss home."

She raised her brows.

"My parents aren't very nice people," I told her.

She sighed. "Who is?"

My thoughts dwelled, more and more, on Mod's girl. She was indentured, she said. She showed me the mark of the dragon on her wrist. She wasn't just a masseuse; she did other work for him, too. But what work, she refused to say, and I didn't want to know.

I wrote on the curves of her back and the canvas of her soul, each letter a pinprick of colour and pain. I gave her a whole tree, roots sinking into hip, jet branches arching up her spine, the crown a watercolour-spray of purple.

"After all this time," I said to her, "I still don't know your name."

She smiled and told me I did. So I called her Wisteria, Wisteria of the Moonlit Garden, Wisteria of ancient longing and transient trysts.

We never met outside of Skin Deep, though sometimes after a session we'd walk along the lake. She said I made her feel uncomfortable, because I saw into her soul. But perhaps it's a pleasurable thing, to be so pierced by another. Because she kept coming, even when the needle-wounds of our previous session had not yet healed. She brought all of her enigmatic love to me, allowing me to pore over her body with my eyes, my ink, my hands. She was a text I could not fathom, different with each read. So unlike me, yet she became a part of me. And when I made her cry my name out in bliss, she said this itself was a form of magic.

It was the oldest power in the world, and she showed me how to cast this spell, with vision, gesture and word, just as she cast it on me.

I rushed out when the first screams started.

In the sky was a monster of my creation, a figment of myth made real. I stood stupefied as the beast with obsidian wings swooped low and snarled, its massive bulk blocking the sun. I glimpsed rows of serrated teeth as from its gaping maw gushed rivers of red.

Shrieks descended into sobs of horror. Smoke welled, dimming the horizon. Flames licked the rooftops beyond the nearest shophouses.

I bolted back in and locked myself upstairs. Wisteria—I should've asked her where she lived. I was pacing by the bed when a glimmer beyond the window froze my heart again.

Behind the trees, the lake rose.

A tideraiser rode the crest of the wave, her body foaming, misting up in spray. Above her the amorphous shape of a windrider flew with his arms outstretched, pushing the tide forward with a squall that shook the trees by the shore. Intermittently the windrider would vaporise into a cloud that pulsed and dissipated and coalesced again into the faint semblance of a man, his storm-grey bowels sparking with lightning as he gathered mass and force. The effect was surreal and jarring, a bruise punched into the middle of a sunlit lake above a frothing wall of teal.

I slammed my windows shut.

The lake crashed down. It spurted up against the rocks and surged through the trees. It struck the walls like thunder. Windows rattled. I fell beside my bed as the floor spasmed.

Then there was only the loud sloosh of water as it gushed through the Claw. Wails rang through the thin walls, and muffled lapping from downstairs told me that the lake was spilling in.

When a smidgen of calm returned, I waded through the mucky water and debris, leaving the door open to let the water drain. It was only knee-deep, thank the gods, but I'd have to throw out most of my furniture.

I thought, vaguely, to search for her. I didn't even have her name, not any that would be recognised. Still, I wandered through the flood, hoping.

All noise whittled down to silence when I turned into Fortune Street, where Mod's house was.

Since the Claw was a gaudy replica of Jewel, all the sunstone and stained-glass buildings held up, but the poor suffered most, as usual. Squatter dwellings sat in sad, soggy ruins. Luckily the gangs had to curb their own penchant for violence; damaged shops meant less to extort.

A shadow passed overhead. The dragon dived down.

Its bulk diminished, wings folding into arms as it metamorphosised into Mod. He rushed into the burned remains of a building with a bellow of such grief that I felt a squeeze of panic—was Wisteria in there, bones crumbling to ash? I stumbled forward, my flapping wet trousers slowing me down.

Mod spotted me as I was scrabbling through the charred heap. "My daughter," he said blankly, almost like a question.

I didn't know what to say. Hesitantly, I reached out to lay a hand on his shoulder. He continued speaking in that same hollow voice, as if he was trying to make sense of the mess he'd made.

"I meant to target Flint Street. Just the Crows' houses. But once I started ..." He shuddered. "I couldn't stop. I wanted to see it all burn. The anger felt good."

His wrath was sudden and terrible. He shoved my hand away and whirled on me, his face contorted. "*You* did this," he snarled, grabbing my collar and lifting me clean off the ground. "You turned me into this—this *monster*." His huge fist shook, and my body shook with it. "*You killed my daughter*," he roared, and a world of anguish flamed into fury as the dragon slithered up his neck.

Something slammed into him from behind. I collapsed with a splash, choking with terror and relief.

The Crows were the oldest, biggest gang in the Claw, and they would not go down easy. They came for him now, their tideraiser from one end of the street and their windrider from another, the two Amari raising their hands to attack. Their bodies dispersed sporadically into spray and vapour, but as their sleeves fell back I glimpsed the Crows' mark on their left wrists.

The windrider's palm struck the air like a slap. A gale shrieked through the street. The tideraiser made another gesture and the flood began to boil.

Mod leapt into the air, great wings unfurling. Fire erupted from his mouth. I flinched, the sudden wave of heat scorching.

No time to run.

But the windrider flicked his wrists, and the flames hit an invisible shield and sputtered out, devoid of oxygen.

The dragon fled. The windrider vaporised, shooting after him. A shadow over the sun—they were gone.

A garish sunset washed over the empty street, turning the water to blood. I wondered how many had survived. The tideraiser must have been thinking along the same lines, because she sighed and lifted her arms again. I shied away, but as water trickled from the surviving houses, I realised she was sweeping out the flood.

"Go home," she snapped, when she caught me staring.

I plodded through the streets until dawn broke the next day and I returned, drenched and muddy, to Skin Deep. I thought I'd never be able to fall asleep but I must have, because I heard Wisteria calling. Her face multiplied before me, dissolving in mist. I saw the tree still half-complete on her back, a blur of scattered petals, colours fading.

For months, I waited. I repaired what I could of Skin Deep, threw out what I couldn't. I thought, then tried not to think, of the monster I'd made. The people Mod had killed. Did he have a choice, or did I rob him of it?

Did it matter? They were still dead.

When Wisteria finally came again, I hid my face so she wouldn't see how I almost wept when I saw her. My tongue felt swollen, blocking my throat, so I turned her around and poured myself into filling in her back.

"It's been chaos," she said. "Mod's pals are dead; the Werms have been fighting among themselves. Now the new boss has called a truce with the Crows. Mod's just biding his time, though—I know him. He'll keep coming until the Crows are destroyed. He'll keep coming for you. Zy, you have to leave."

I focused on the contour of her shoulders, using them to suggest a hint of mist.

She turned to stare at me.

"It's not your fault, Zy. You couldn't have known. The anger was in him all along, and it's far easier to blame others for our own flaws."

I shook my head. "I reduced him," I rasped, "to a flat image. A one-dimensional idea. I took away his capacity for change."

Thoughtfully, she studied her arm, letting ripples of blue-green play beneath her fingertips. "No image is one-dimensional. No one is incapable of change."

I etched in the last few branches.

"With Mod gone," I said, "does this mean you're free?"

"I still serve the Werms—or whoever commands them."

I'd tried to work slowly, but the end was inevitable. Shu's ink was running out. I only had black left, and it was down to the dregs.

"Why do you hide them?" I asked later, as we lay tangled in each other's limbs on my bed upstairs. I traced the soft contour of her arm, the peacock plumes hidden beneath her silver-birch skin.

She glanced away. "To survive," she said flatly. Then she looked at me and decided to trust. "I belonged to the Thousand-Flower Court. I couldn't let people see … who I was."

"And now?"

"Mod bought my contract a year ago. He needed someone charming but forgettable. I get close to powerful people and make them talk. Sometimes I threaten, sometimes I kill. So I'm faceless, nameless"—she rolled over, pecked me on the lips—"except with you."

I didn't ask how many she'd killed.

Another troubling thought struck me. "You should've told me. I wouldn't have—" I gestured at her back, the punctures I'd made. Wounds not yet healed.

"No, I wanted the truth you saw."

"Was there any … Wisteria?"

Her smile grew sad. "Many. There was Jasmine, Sakura, Orchid … Only the wealthiest can afford a Wisteria. It's Ištara's flower, after all." She put a hand over mine. "But they were never like me. This"—she gestured at her back—"is your Wisteria."

I laced my fingers in hers. Her hand was calloused, used to hard work, unlike mine. "Flee with me. Or … the Crown could use you—"

"I have had enough of being used. Besides …" She sat up and touched her foot. A rune appeared, blood-red and pulsing, knife-cuts etched into her right sole. She sighed. "It keeps me within the Claw. Two years, Mod promised. Then I am free."

"You trust him? He's ruled by anger."

"My contract with the Crows was ninety-nine years. I was twelve when they kidnapped me. They didn't want to break my skin, so they kicked my legs open and filled me with crushed firefruit. Again and again until I performed. Mod offered me hope."

That glint in her eyes.

"And vengeance," I murmured.

She was quiet.

"Thank you," she said softly, "for your gift. It's made me a little more whole. I could never have touched you without it, could never have loved. And now I've found a way to use it—as a weapon." She raised her chin. "Tonight, I return to the Thousand-Flower Court."

"As a spy," I spat, "dressed as the goddess of love."

Her gaze on me was steel. "They'll see me and love me. Then I'll kill the man who took my innocence."

Nothing left but pitch-black stains on the tips of my needles. Nothing I could do to save the woman I loved.

I pressed my black-tipped needles into my skin, on the inside of my wrist. I wanted to give myself twin spears, but all I succeeded in making was a meaningless smudge, like the shadow of a falling leaf.

That night, silently, I followed her.

I slipped through the throng—the gamblers and revellers of Hogshead, the silk-robed gentry in their palanquins, into the vine-wreathed arcades and stained-glass atria of the Thousand-Flower Court.

No one noticed; my name was Shadow.

Invisible, bodiless, I lurked in a corner as she danced, lilac silks streaming around her willow frame. On her exposed back was the tree I'd carved, petals eddying as she twirled. I saw eyes bright with desire, men's and women's both, knees weak before this shining Ištara. When she was done a profound hush fell over the hall, as though her dance had been sacred. Then the whispers:

Beautiful

ah, unrivalled

How much do you think—

Wisteria, wisteria, her Name susurrated through the hall, rising to a crescendo as the audience shouted their bids. But the Court was owned by Raf Gola, king of the Crows, and if Raf wanted a Flower, no one opposed him.

And how could he not want her? That night, everyone was touched by her light. Perhaps they felt, as I did when I watched her, that the lines between all souls softened, and in that catch of breath we could break free of ourselves. Even Raf, I think, fell a little in love with her.

Already he had marked her: three crows on the left wrist. With Mod gone, the rune that bound her in the Claw for two years, a contract binding in flesh, could now be owned by him. How much had Raf paid the Werms for it?

He took her by the elbow, two henchmen trailing behind. We meandered up a spiralling staircase and into a cavernous chamber, high-ceilinged, marble-floored, walls of stained glass backlit by the balcony's lanterns.

Raf left his men guarding the door. I skulked in the darkness as she pulled him to her.

They lit no candles. The windows threw light around like a prism, the bed a luminous altar. He lay her down, and her body moulded itself to his like mercury. And as he buried his face in her neck, she reached up, slowly, to pull a slender blade from the voluminous whorls of her hair.

It was my fault. I had bound her with a name inscribed on flesh. For as the dragon could not control his rage, so Wisteria, Ištara, goddess of love, could not kill.

Their bodies rose and fell together, rose and fell, and the knife hovered behind his back, catching colour like a butterfly wing.

Then Raf sat up to turn her over, and grim realisation darkened his features while beneath him Wisteria still reached for him, lips parted, cheeks flushed. Was she struggling, as Love clashed with Vengeance? Did those twin spears flicker on her arm, before his cloak cast a pall over her?

The shadows fell uselessly around them.

I could only watch as he pried the knife from her fingers, and tenderly, regretfully—as if it were a waste to kill such beauty— plunged it into her heart.

When the door clicked shut I materialised, cradling her in my arms; too stunned to weep, too scared to scream. Her eyes were closed, her mouth still open as if in bliss.

A terraformer could've saved her.

But I was a Namer with no ink, a gangly boy with too-soft skin, barely a man. What could I do against the king of the Crows?

What could I do, as Shadow? I followed him.

I took his sight so that he staggered, wild-eyed and raving as he crashed down the stairs. His men shouted in confusion and hurried to support him, and I blinded them, too. I thought that was all I could do. I had Named myself. I was only shadow.

But I was pure grief, mad with it, and I found more.

Shadow lengthened, gained form and texture, became a cloud. The men ran in panic as the cloud grew, filling the halls, suffocating.

It was still just smoke, immaterial.

Then Cloud became Shroud, and Shroud wrapped itself tight around Raf's body, revelling in his muffled screams. It dragged him through the air and over the city, binding his face like a second skin. And when it reached the mirror-dark lake, it shoved him in.

His throat opened. Water gushed in. I felt his body buck.

As his dark robes sank beneath me, I rose, swelling gently with the last bubbles of his breath. And I mourned, for it was not only Wisteria I had lost.

Summer again, a sultry moon. A black cat darts past my window.

The door swings open and a boy enters Skin Deep, his features vaguely familiar, his slanting eyes impossibly green. He walks straight up to me as if he knows me and hands me a jar of tarry ink. "Another one for the road?" he says.

I frown.

"Shu's ink." A smirk flirts about his lips, and I begin to like him, despite my bemusement. "I found her and persuaded her to give me the formula."

The boy grows serious. "Raf's dead; the rune no longer holds me. We can leave the Claw together, go somewhere Mod won't find us." He looks around, lips quirking up again. "You need new furniture, anyway."

Lips I have kissed.

She stands before me with a naughty gleam, a strange boy with scruffy hair but whose aura I recognise nonetheless. "How—" I am lost for words.

She spreads her arms and shows me. Her skin bursts to life in a riot of colour, diaphanous panes shifting and overlapping; picture after picture layered one on another, saturating every spot her hands can reach. The Creator with his blue-green plumes, the Destroyer with his spears. There were Lorétheian gods too: a cat with dangerous eyes, typifying the Trickster whose boyish form she'd taken; a tree bowed like an offering, its crown laden with wisteria. And more, not just gods but symbols, all runes in their own right.

For a long time, I stare. Then I understand. After all, isn't that what a god is—a rune, a word-image of transformative power? As Trickster, she evaded hell. As Warrior, she wrestled back to life. As Creator, she would forge a new beginning, and as Love, she would do it with me.

"I have many names," they say, laughing, "many faces, many lives. We are what we make ourselves—so we picked our selves up, and climbed out of hell."

They say this like it's the easiest thing in the world.

"What about vengeance?" I ask. "I robbed it from you."

Wisteria smiles, their eyes the calm of evening. "There will be justice. But if all men are equal, then no one alone can be its arbiter. Vengeance was never mine to take."

I frown, incredulous. "If I hadn't killed him, you would have let him go?"

"Ah, so it was you."

I swallow. Wisteria tilts their head, searching for the words.

"For so long," they murmur, "we carried vengeance in our heart. It was a crushing weight, consuming, corrosive. It did not let me live."

"You would forget all he's done to you? What about all he would have done to others?"

Wisteria spreads their hands. "There is law."

I shake my head. "The laws are decided by the powerful."

"Should I then claim power for myself?"

I bite my lip.

They try again. They come close to take my hand, placing a palm over my chest. "Listen."

My heart leaps to meet their fingers.

"When Love looked into the eyes of her neighbour," Wisteria whispers, their gaze on me clear and penetrating, "she saw his soul—and it was indistinguishable from hers. She saw the violence of his parents and his grandparents and further back still, experienced the whole web of actions and consequences that shaped him finally into the monster that killed her, again and again, within himself. In a single breath, Love lived his life, and he could be her enemy no longer."

On their skin a wash of purple; in their eyes a glimmer of tears. Then they grow strong and hard and the twin spears flash like lightning in their hands, even as wisterias cascade across the ground. "Yet Love was also every soul he had destroyed, and we were still the girl whose life he'd stolen. Justice must be done—but we didn't want it done that way. So we destroyed the hate within ourselves. And then …" They turn away to face the window, moonlight silvering their cheeks. "We went to hell."

I watch, entranced, as petals spill over my feet.

"We felt our body return like a cloak over our soul, gathering itself from the ash it had become. We could be anything we wanted. We were a cat. We were a boy. We were a woman. We were more."

"But Raf …" I cannot let it go. I have to justify myself. "You understand, don't you? He had to be punished."

Wisteria lowers their head. "I understand."

When they speak again, their voice is soft with sorrow, and their words sound slow and distant, like a priestly parable, or a storyteller's tale of far-off lands.

"We saw him, on our way out. The king of the Crows on hell's barren plains, digging himself into a pit. He could have walked out any time he wanted, but he kept digging. Perhaps he'll dig forever. Or perhaps he'll find his way through the hell of his own making, someday understanding enough to turn around." Wisteria sighs, a breath like many winds. "Who, after all, is innocent? We are none of us alone. We'll all pay, in some way, for the blood on our hands."

I think of the body of the man I killed, rotting in the deep. A baby burning in the ruins, a man possessed by rage. A boy whose name I should have known.

Wisteria turns back to me. Their eyes are bright and sharp again, irises the jewel-green of spring. "Yet," they say, and the echo of their voices fill the room, fill my heart, as a myriad faces veil one another, and grin. "Yet through it all, we'll live."

I gather them all in Shadow, and leap into the night.

Celine Low is a writer, painter, dancer and educator in Singapore and India. Her poetry, fiction and art have appeared in many literary magazines. She has ghostwritten thrillers, enrichment curricula and recipe books for fairies. Celine holds an MA in English Literature from the National University of Singapore where she did her dissertations on Tolkien and on the intersection of contemporary literature and architecture

Play It on Repeat

Brianna Suazo

Play It on Repeat

Penny knew going to lunch with Leo was probably a bad idea. She really didn't have the time and preferred eating at her desk. Her boss's words kept bouncing around in her head. "Your argument is good, but it's too conventional," she had said. "You need to look at the case from every angle." Penny knew it was good criticism, useful, but it only made her feel more stuck.

To make matters worse, the sandwich place where she was meeting Leo was seven blocks from her firm. For the entire walk, she could feel the back of her pumps digging all the way through her tights and pulling away the top layer of ankle skin.

When she got there, he was loitering off to the side of the line, pressing his back against the list of artisanal cheeses. He didn't see her at first, he was staring at something in his hands. She angled herself so that he would spot her and waved.

He jumped, suddenly aware of her presence. "Hey, Penny!" he said with a small wave of his hand that hung stiffly at his side. He looked pretty much the same as she remembered, wearing a worn-out t-shirt, gray beanie, and dark jeans. He even had a slightly shorter version of his classic floppy, swept aside haircut.

They bought their sandwiches and sat at a table too close to the soda machine. He asked how she was doing. She gave him the short version; her move to the city after law school and how much she admired the partners at her firm. She started to talk about how she wanted to work on more domestic violence cases when she realized that, despite staring intently at her, he didn't seem to be listening all that closely.

Penny had that tight feeling in the back of her throat when she didn't know how to handle an awkward conversation.

"Are you still working in sound engineering?" she asked.

"Uh, no, not exactly. Well, sometimes. I'm mostly doing design stuff now, for like, video games and visualizations."

"Oh wow, that sounds really cool! Are you working for a studio or…?"

"No, no, mostly just freelancing."

"Oh, that's awesome. Have you done stuff for anyone I might've heard of?"

"Um, no, probably not."

The din of the voices around them rose up again to fill the silence. Penny was relieved to see Leo was almost done with his ham on rye. She ate her wrap faster, but not so fast he would notice.

"So, what are you doing in town?" she asked over the married couple debating the health of diet cola. "You said something in your text about visiting friends, but I don't really know who from Point Hugo lives out here."

"Oh, you know. Rick, Shelley, Fisher," he trailed off.

"Tyler Fisher? You guys get along now?"

"Oh, uh, yeah. We worked together at the diner out by I40 for a bit after I moved back, so we hang out."

"You worked at Pecans?" She couldn't help but laugh. "I'm surprised they even let you back in! We used to be complete little jerks there."

His face lit up into a grin. "God, yeah, remember when we tried to cheat the system on the unlimited pancakes?"

"Yes, and when they cut us off you stood up on the table and Rick started playing the Star-Spangled Banner on the harmonica?"

"It was beautiful!" he said.

"And your speech, what did you--?"

"Liberty and pancakes for all!" He put his fists in the air, the same show of victory he gave when the manager of Pecans had kicked them out so quickly, he forgot to give them the check. "God, don't you miss all that?"

"It was pretty fun," she said, "life was simpler back then." She got up to throw away her wrapper. He hastily got up, too. They walked out the side entrance by the patio, abandoned for winter. She glanced at her phone. 12:33. She had to get back.

"I knew it," Leo said, shaking his head with a small, satisfied smile. He suddenly pulled her close, toward the alley behind them. She could feel his hand brush through her hair. "I knew you were still in there."

"What? Leo I--"

Before she could get another word out, she suddenly felt dizzy and out of place. Leo's hand went back to his side, but she didn't feel it.

Then suddenly they were back sitting in the sandwich shop. Everyone in the restaurant started moving backward, too fast to be real. She distantly felt herself stand up, but it was all wrong. She walked backward out the restaurant and moments later she was walking through the door of her office building and on the train and outside of her apartment and the whole time it was going faster and faster and faster with a faint whirring sound in the background like a VHS tape playing in jittery reverse. At some point, there was only colored light that might have been rooms or people blurring past her so quickly she felt sick and out of breath.

Then, just as it was getting so fast that Penny couldn't bear it, everything stopped moving. She was vaguely aware that she was laying on the ground and even more vaguely aware that someone-- slowly coming into focus as Leo--was standing over her.

She thought for a moment that she had passed out on the sidewalk. But there was a ceiling above her. It was far away, metallic, and industrial. And there was this loud, crashing music that sounded like it was right next to her. She closed her eyes tight and opened them again. Leo looked different, too. His hair was longer and even floppier, he was dressed slightly differently than before, and he was skinnier. He kept looking down at her and then back at his hands with a big, goofy smile on his face that she couldn't even begin to comprehend.

She pushed herself up by her elbows and realized the floor was wet and sticky. There were people shuffling around her, endless legs and feet nearly stepping on her. The music was somehow getting louder. The tune even sounded familiar.

Leo bent down next to her, still grinning like an idiot. "Okay, Penny, listen to me and please don't freak out," he said, shouting over the crowd.

She knew how she knew the song. It was that band that Rick's cousin was in that they were obsessed with in high school. They practically had to beg them to come play in their town, in that dingy old warehouse that was owned by somebody's dad who wouldn't ask questions. The stage was barely visible from where she was sitting but it looked like them. She could have sworn they broke up back when--

"Pen, can you hear me?" Leo yelled again, interrupting her train of thought. He put his hand on her shoulder and she realized that the strands of her hair over it were dark blue.

"This can't be right," she finally said.

"So, uh, long story short," he said, "I can time travel."

Penny stumbled to her feet and immediately ran through the crowd away from him.

She could hear him calling behind her, but she kept running, pushing her way through the mass of people. Some of the faces that looked back at her were familiar; old classmates gave her looks that ranged from annoyed to concerned.

She raced into the warehouse's bathroom and clutched the sides of one of the dingy sinks, not sure if she was going to pass out or throw up. A startled, disheveled version of her sixteen-year-old self stared back at her with bloodshot eyes from across the mirror.

"Penny, are you in here?" a voice she recognized called from the door.

"Vera?" she called back in disbelief.

Her best friend stepped into the bathroom, and she still half-expected to see the tired mom who sent her Christmas cards every year. But no, it was bright-eyed, pink-streaked-haired Vera.

Without thinking, Penny just ran over and hugged her. All of this was still completely insane, but Vera would understand, they would figure it out together. The embrace caught Vera by surprise and the contents of her red cup sloshed onto Penny's arm.

"Oh, sorry, sorry," Vera said, grabbing paper towels from the barely-functional dispenser. "Leo said you got really claustrophobic and panicky all the sudden and I wanted to make sure you were okay."

Penny wrinkled her nose at the smell coming from her arm. "What were you drinking?"

"Rum and Coke," Vera said, dabbing her arm with the towels. "Sorry, hopefully the cops don't show up, 'cause frankly you're going to smell like a bar fight."

"Hey, is she okay?" Leo called in from the hallway.

"Yeah!" Vera called back. More quietly to Penny, she said, "he should probably drive you home. You look like you're going to be sick."

Penny nodded. "Yeah, tell him I'll be right out, okay?"

The moment Vera left, Penny climbed out through the window.

She hurried away from the warehouse. She could see the row of lights from the smattering of neighborhoods. She thought of going home, to her parents' house rather. But she couldn't bring herself to go that way. It would make it too real. Instead, she walked the other way with no particular destination in mind.

She found herself in front of Sunrise Creek. She sat down on the bank and let the water lap at her mud-caked combat boots. It was the same water she used to splash around in as a kid. A soft summer breeze rustled the trees. She hoped to make some sense of everything in the quiet, but all she found was a feeling settling in her chest that this was happening.

After a while, she felt a buzz in her pocket. She pulled out a chunky, black flip phone and opened it. After a bit of fumbling through menus, she found the new text.

'@Pecans. Plz come, Ill explain-L'

In front of her across the creek, there was an endless expanse of pitch-black farmland. She glanced back behind her, at the lights of the town. Then she looked left, where she could barely see the single glowing sign out by the highway. She sighed, stood up, and headed towards it.

She slid into the booth where he was waiting for her. "Take me back to the present."

"Hello to you, too," he said with a hint of amusement. "I got you a coffee."

"This isn't funny, Leo. I'm still trying to wrap my head around the fact that it's even possible, but I know it sure as hell isn't funny. Take me back, *now*."

He looked down at his shoes. "I…I can't."

"*What?*" she shouted. Several people turned to look at the two of them.

"Please, Penny, lower your voice," Leo whispered.

She ignored him and said even louder, "What do you mean, you can't?"

"I can only go backwards!"

She was on the verge of tears. "Why? Why the hell would you make me come back here?"

"We were happy here, Pen. Don't you remember?"

She let out a short, bitter laugh. "Yeah, being an angsty, pissed-off teenager in a tiny town was the highlight of my life."

"So, what," he said, suddenly accusatory, "you want to go back to being that bland, blazer-wearing lawyer?"

"*Excuse* me?"

"You used to be so interesting. God, you're the reason *I'm* interesting. What the hell happened?"

"Are you kidding me right now? Leo, I grew up!" she could feel her voice getting higher, a tell that she thought she had learned to control in law school. "I like my life. I worked my ass off for that life, and I make a difference."

Leo wrinkled his nose. "Filing contracts?"

She wanted to defend herself. She wanted to tell him the entire story of the time she won her first case, about the first client who sobbed in her arms, about the time a powerful attorney tried to intimidate her and failed. Or hell, the time she drove across the country by herself, the three times she had fallen in love, and how she still jammed to Knife Parade and Time Assassins on the train.

She bit her tongue, though. Leo didn't have any right to the person she was now. Instead, she just said, "get me out of here."

"I'm sorry, I should've asked first, I can't control it sometimes. You'll come around, I know you will," he said, softening his tone again and giving her that little half-smile that used to make her swoon. "This is the real you."

She felt like a trapped animal. She wanted to scrape at the walls of the diner, then at anything she could find in the woods outside, until she found some hole that would get her back home.

And then she found something. Not a hole, exactly, but a new angle.

"Did you know that Vera's father was an alcoholic?" she asked him.

He squinted at her, confused at this sudden turn in the conversation. "No, why?

She wasn't looking back at him. Instead, she took to examining the table and the coffee cup in front of her. Everything looked and felt perfect, especially the imperfection. There was a chip on the rim of one of the cups. She ran her thumb against it while she spoke. "Yeah, everyone thought Mr. Garrett was her dad, because he adopted her before they moved here. Her real dad died when she was little. She swore she'd never end up like him. She faked drinking at parties for years." Finally, she looked at him. A small, disbelieving smile crept across her face as the implications finally dawned on her. "You had *no idea*, did you, Leo?"

"Penny, what are you ta--"

"No, no, you shut up," she interrupted. "We're not in 2007, we're not even in Point Hugo! Time travel?" she scoffed. "God, you really tried to pass off that *thing* in there, casually holding a fucking rum and Coke in her hand, as my best friend. What, did you think I was going to go home to your creepy sims versions of my family and I wouldn't notice? How long did you think this was going to last?"

He was staring at her with wide eyes and she couldn't tell if the expression on his face was anger or fear.

"You were always so smart. I mean, obviously, this," she said while gesturing to everything around, "is incredible. I don't know how you did it and maybe once I would have cared. But Leo, for all your brilliance, you've always been so blind. You know why? Because you're so deeply, stupidly self-absorbed."

His hands balled into fists and she could hear that VHS whirring again, somewhere in the distance. Out of the corner of her eye, she saw a stool at the counter dissolve into nothing.

"What," she dug in further, "you couldn't build me, too? You seem to have no problem making creepy little puppets of everyone else."

Nothing disappeared this time, and she caught a shy half-smile on Leo's face. "You were too...I don't know. You were too alive."

His smile, along with the neon wall clock by the counter, disintegrated when he saw Penny's look of disgust.

"Penny, please. I'm sorry I lied, but you have no idea how hard I've worked on this. Stay here with me."

"No."

Her coffee cup dissolved too, and so did the man sitting two tables away.

"I love you," he said.

She was surprised when she felt a sudden pang of sadness. "No, you don't," she said softly, putting her hand over his. "You love your version of me."

The entire diner started to chip away, bit by bit, individual pixels flickered to black. And for a moment, they were both falling into nothingness. And with a jarring sudden jerk, she was back in the alley by the sandwich shop, face down on the concrete.

She was shaking and dizzy, and suddenly felt a sharp pain in the back of her head. Leo's hand was still on top of it. He was slumped against the building, eyes closed. She slowly lifted his hand up, pulling a long needle out of her head in the process. It hurt like hell; black spots formed in her vision as she pulled it out. There was a chip with circuitry taped to his hand, attached to another needle in the vein to his wrist. A series of wires, thicker than the one by the needle, went into his sleeve. With his head bent down, she could see that the wires led up his neck and disappeared into the back of his skull, lined up from ear to ear.

Penny still felt woozy, and it took a few seconds to look away from Leo's crumpled form. When she did, she realized three things at once. The first was that the time on her phone, now laying on the ground, read 12:35. The second, that a crowd was forming around them, including a woman wearing a nametag for the sandwich shop. She was on the phone, probably calling 911. Third, she realized that Leo wasn't breathing.

━━━◆◆◆━━━

Brianna Suazo writes in Boulder, Colorado. She has been published in Spider Mirror Literary Journal, Havok, and Toasted Cheese Literary Journal. In addition to writing, she enjoys exploring bookstores, hiking, and annoying her loved ones with inane trivia.

Subscribe

If you've enjoyed these stories and want more, you can buy single issues or subscribe to *Wyldblood Magazine* at **www.wyldblood.com/magazine**

Every three months in print or digital download.

Anthologies

Check out our other fine anthologies at

www.wyldblood.com/shop,

from Amazon or from bookstores

Print or digital download.

Twitter - @WyldbloodPress
Facebook - www.facebook.com/wyldbloodpress
Website - www.wyldblood.com
Newsletter - http://eepurl.com/haa4Zn
Email - contact@wyldblood.com

www.wyldblood.com

WYLDBLOOD